Robert Gary McGuiness was born in Bay Shore, New York, on February 8, 1954. He graduated from Smithtown Central High School in 1972. After school he travelled west to Arizona and eventually to California, where he has lived since 1976. He was an active part of the "back to land" movement and homesteaded off the grid in Northern California. He has two children, three wonderful grandchildren and a dog named Marbles.

My mother and father:

Margaret Jean (Reidy) McGuiness (31 December 1924 – 17 August 2019)

Robert Eugene McGuiness (6 February 1925 – 15 July 2011)

Robert McGuiness

THE ATTENUATING PURITAN

AUSTIN MACAULEY PUBLISHERS™

LONDON • CAMBRIDGE • NEW YORK • SHARJAH

Ordering Information
Quantity sales: Special discounts are available on quantity purchases by corporations, associations, and others. For details, contact the publisher at the address below.

Publisher's Cataloging-in-Publication data
McGuiness, Robert
The Attenuating Puritan

ISBN 9798889102663 (Paperback)
ISBN 9798889102670 (Hardback)
ISBN 9798889102687 (ePub e-book)

Library of Congress Control Number: 2023920562

www.austinmacauley.com/us

First Published 2024
Austin Macauley Publishers LLC
40 Wall Street, 33rd Floor, Suite 3302
New York, NY 10005
USA

mail-usa@austinmacauley.com
+1 (646) 5125767

To my children Jewel and Bob for the perpetual inspiration and motivation. To my grandchildren, Yarah, Indira and Ave who provide firsthand a lens in which visions of our collective futures come into focus. To all the children of the world, for you belong to this. And to all the future generations, for this belongs to you. I would also like to thank the many hands at Austin Macauley Publishers for bringing this project to fruition, including but not limited to the Editorial Department, the Production Department, the Art Department, the Marketing and Promotion Departments, and to all those involved. Specifically, I am grateful to Aaliyah Gerena, Delainey Hanson, Jennifer Lane, Ben List, Liam Brown, Stephen Lawrence, Otis Feld, and Clara Jenning.

Upon awakening, mother was dead. The toddler shook her and poked his finger in her eye; she remained unresponsive. He began to cry and grabbed her arm, but she was too heavy to move. Sobbing, he grew angry and began to hit her and crying hysterically, he punched her with all his little might, …and ever so faintly, her heart started once again to beat. Upon awakening, I found I was the toddler, the earth was mother, but the nightmare continued.

I grew up at the bottom of a hill that was repeatedly sprayed with one of the two ingredients that made agent orange: 2,4-D and 2,4,5-T. We had a shallow well, being, we were not too far from sea level, and though the geologic engineers and hydrologists asserted our water was distinct and separate from the surrounding surface water and there was no concern about contamination, I was borderline autistic, ADHD, and on meds by the first grade. Mother's milk was menthol, and I had tainted formula on the weekends at grandma's. We would ride bikes behind the trucks spraying DDT for the mosquitoes, peddling like dogs, sucking wind trying to keep up, and then eat the unwashed fruit from the roadside orchards. A few years later, I just assumed all altar boys were on psych meds. I went cold turkey and got off them all together. At first, I had trouble deciding, no I did not, well maybe a little, had difficulties making up my mind, nah… I think it seems I am doing better these days, sort of, but I still have trouble, like decision-making flashbacks, they kind of cause anxiety. Some days I just crack and go a little nuts, I think. Space is good, and quiet is good wherever you can find it.

When I was about eight years old, a tanker truck rolled over and dumped its contents. Though I never made it to the site, the product found its way a couple of miles to the pond where we would play. Trickled down the little stream and made a major fish kill. Thousands of fish in the pond pushed to shore, belly up. The sludge continued for another mile and a half to another pond, which was a much larger body of water, and another seemingly smaller fish kill. Then onto another creek and eventually to the river. Three creeks, two ponds, and a river in the clutches of death from one tanker truck of some oil product. I never gave any thought to the driver, never gave any thought to what exactly the chemicals were or their long-term effects. Ignorance is bliss, but I lost mine to the massive fish kills.

Thinking back, I think the first time I had to question if a food I was eating was safe was when they announced mercury in the tuna fish. I loved tuna fish. Before that, I believed that if you said grace, you could eat anything. I still say grace, but I am weary of packaged foods.

As I wandered aimlessly for a time, hiking, hitchhiking, and hopping trains, I grew a bit more introverted. The Lord's work became paramount, and I was determined to give Mother a makeover. Soon the Lord had commanded all my attention. These hands were his; these feet were his; my loyalty and devotion, undeniable, unquestionable, and I waited for further instruction. His voice was loud, maybe not so clear, and I was all pumped up with nowhere to go. Forty years in the desert under a mumbling God. In the drainage ditch on the side of the road, billions of thoughts rushed by. The gurgling spoke in numerous tongues, many of which went unrecognized; some of the words of men, some were the words of God. The runoff from just a few hundred feet of highway dispersed enough oil to paint rainbows in the quiet pools on the periphery of the main flow. The colors painted a picture of death and fish bellies and salted a traumatizing laceration of my youth. The sedges appeared oily and this I believed to be part of the natural process. It took great restraint not to try to clean them and their proximal rainbows.

I pondered myself, a myriad of dots, and an ego that fixed on connecting every last one. That chemical self, like the unrosined bow, could not produce the tune, but not for lack of effort. Some days were easier than others, accepting the turtle pace of the attenuator. Most often, days came with a dreadful urgency manifesting and a quick time march paced my janitorial duties. As I prayed for direction, I was graced with thoughts and images of Brother Nut. As I sank beneath the load I carried, be it air pollution, water pollution, plastics, endocrine disruptors, glyphosate, and the mitochondrial protein folding dilemma, the global issues at times seemed too overwhelming to address. Just then, a spark of hope on the horizon…Brother Nut vacuuming the polluted air in China and making bricks. A kindred spirit, another attenuator, and then there were two. I gave thanks! I waited, waited for a sign. As the runoff chortled, Flint, Michigan, surfaced. The situation in Flint was about the lead in the water, and my energy levels were high as I received my new assignment.

I would miss the late season foraging at and near the Love Canal. I was getting sick and depressed squatting there for the last forty days or so. Dark spots appeared on my skin, and multiple new, festering lesions broke out across my body. My liver pained and I was continually nauseous, and I believed I was saturated and could not attenuate any more at this time at this location. My initial plan was to hitchhike to Flint, taking a few days off to fast, and then cleanse. I knew the lead levels were high and that it would be challenging and risky. Cleaning all of Flint was not real but targeting certain waters was certainly possible. The plan solidified in my mind…I was to systematically drink the holy water in as many of the churches as I could, attenuating the lead and rescuing the Lord's flock. I was well aware of the fact that I would grow sickly and stupid, maybe below moron clear to idiot. I wrote notes to myself in an effort to keep a set of keys back to my kingdom, reminding me of who I am and what purpose I had in Flint and in life. I wrote words of faith and words of hope, words of strength and manifesting encouragement, knowing full well they might be for naught.

As I held my thumb out on the interstate, I remembered seeing a man walking bearing a large cross, and on the bottom of the vertical post had a wheel attached to it, so it would kind of roll along with him. He did not want to carry the cross because that would be too much like Christ, and he let you know he was not Christ…just a reminder of him. I first saw him near Winnipeg, in the Canadian plains west of there. Then, years later, along the coast in California, next along Highway 40 in Arizona. One could not help but to wonder about him. What exactly was his mission? Was he just another s(t)crolling advertisement? Who, what, or how was this behavior elicited? Should he be flogging himself? Should he be picking up trash? I do not know; though our paths crossed, I never got to know the man, but I appreciate him. Here I am on the side of the road, flaunting the robe of repentance, hoping but not wasting prayer on avoiding law enforcement, and trying my best to look normal.

The surplice was pure white, save for the bloody anal stigmata. A deep conical hood fell behind, the sleeves flared and loose. The puritan would joke that it is a tech tunicle, as it was smarter than a smart phone, complete with alpha brain wave monitoring and lie detector functions. The entirety of the robe was pixelated and equipped with a plethora of apps and features, such as heating and cooling, cameras with near endless memory, which could record and document one's entire life. The robe would monitor heart rate, respiration, blood oxygen levels, perspiration, and other physiological subtleties. The robe was capable of doing blood tests and could detect the presence of heat shock proteins, necessary for any attenuator. The robe would broadcast one's devotion to God, as it would pixelate should one lie, always responding to information received and, within a set of parameters, sending feedback. If a small untruth were revealed, a pixel would turn black; if the stress-triggering events were greater, then an entire swatch would blacken. Awareness of one's behavior, especially sin, would immediately be admonished.

The sun was bright, the air crisp, and the sky blue between the scattered clouds. There was not a thought in my head, which was just a wind-kissed ocarina droning an earthen ohm. There was enough duty remaining to be on task waiting for the eventual ride, and in the couple hundred square feet around me, I managed half a small sack of trash. It was not all that long before a newer Chevy pickup truck pulled over. It was gray slate colored. I saw the baby on board sign in the back window, and my thoughts muted the ocarina. As I approached the vehicle, I heard her say, "Hurry up, get in. I am not supposed to stop along here."

"Thanks for the lift," I said.

"My name is Angela," she said.

I am sure glad you stopped. I tried to make conversation, and not realizing how socially inept I was, I bombarded her with banal excess and cornball suave. If I had to guess, I would have said she was thirty-eight. She had thin, dirty blonde hair and big blue eyes. The truck matched her outfit: an unbuttoned green flannel, a tee shirt underneath, jeans, and boots. The boots were more hiking boots than work boots, but I assumed they were work boots for her.

"I am the attenuating puritan; I try not to color out of the lines, but with so many colors and diminished fine motor skills, you will often hear me asking for forgiveness," I told her.

She laughed, and I did not know if she was with me or at me. The whites on the top of her eyes let me know her hair was too tight. Within the first few miles, I learned she had lost custody of her kids and had tried to kill her husband or ex, whatever he was. She managed to work herself up into a shrew in a fraction of a second, apologized, and then oozed an innocent demureness. Something about her had my robe pixelating.

"How far are you going?" I asked.

"Just a little past Cleveland," she answered.

"Cool, I don't want to spend too much time in Ohio; it seems the Lord loses sight of me there," I said truthfully.

"Well, I am actually going to Sandusky. Do you know where that is?" she asked.

"No, not really; I have heard of it."

"It is just about an hour west and still up on the lake," she told me.

"How far is that from Flint?" I asked her.

"I'm not sure, but probably about four hours of driving time," she responded.

"If I get rides, I should make it there tonight," I said to myself out loud.

I told her the Puritans did the Lord's work cleaning the Garden of Eden. The work was exhausting and took a toll physically, emotionally, and spiritually. These sores are from working at the Love Canal. I usually pray and cleanse, and I have been able to heal miraculously fast. I am praying I do now. The Lord has always had my back.

"I'll be praying for you too," she said, "and if no one has told you, thank you for your work," she added.

She put on some music, some kind of woman-empowering pop-rock with an "always me" country whine to it. She sang right along, then went on to tell me she was going to get her kids back. There were three of them from nine years old to two years old. Same regimen, different state. Drug and alcohol classes, anger management and parenting classes, and, of course, checking back in with the courts and social services. To me, she seemed too together for all that shit. One mandated reporter and the parties over. It was probably the ex that filed. I did not ask where the kids were now. She kept on singing.

Before long, we were in Sandusky, and she pulled over at a gas station. She gave me her number and told me to call if I was back in the area. I told her I had neither a number nor an address, but I would call her sometime and let her know what was going on.

"I'd like that," she said.

"I hope you get your kids back…children belong with their mothers. Stay with the program; it will go by fast. Do not give them one reason to drag it out or to fail. Thanks again for the ride. Peace and Love." When the next car pulled over, I noticed Michigan plates and was feeling fortunate, hopefully getting into the right state. It was a black BMW about five years old…I think, but I did not really know. The kid driving was getting back to school in Ann Arbor. He drove fast and did not seem too concerned about getting pulled over.

"I am Michael," he said.

"I am the Attenuating Puritan," I told him.

He pulled out a good-sized joint and lit it, hitting it once and exhaling and hitting it again. "Here," he said as he passed it over to me.

The attenuators' work is never done. I recognized the smell and the taste and told him I had not hit a joint like that since I was in northern California. "Some type of 'chem dawg?" I asked.

"Pretty good you could pick that out," he said. "It is actually Alien Dawg, and I got it from my boy out in 'Cali," He continued.

I thought I could clean that up, but it knocked me down, and I stayed stupefied for the next two hours, ending up in Ann Arbor and he was hurrying me out of the car. I thanked him for the ride, and he laughed at me for not handling his weed too well. He told me it was a pretty cheap bus ticket to get up to Flint, and I asked where the bus station was. He said, "Get back in; I can drop you off there." Next, I was boarding a Greyhound for Flint. I am sure I knew Michael from somewhere.

I decided that all the people on all the buses were the same people, and you could not tell them apart unless you talked to them. I was the only one who did not belong on a bus. The chick that sat next to me did not want to go where she was going and was desperately seeking an alternative. It seemed she was well versed and must have been a frequent flier; she probably logged a million miles or more. The old woman across the aisle was breathing hard and snorting with discontent as she watched the younger displaying her feathers. I thought they must have shared this ride a thousand times…what did I know?

I thought about truth and lies. How lies could be attenuated, and through the prolonged process, the truth would emerge. The truth could not be attenuated because when it was drawn out to a point…it was still the truth. I thought of George Washington and how he could never tell a lie. I am sure he did at some point in his life, but as a leader of people, which is a necessary stance and direction in which the populous need to be moving. Today, the media, politicians, lawmakers, and judges waste time and money as attenuators sorting out the lies their cohorts have sown. When it comes to making money…or at least spending taxpayer monies lying is Americas newest renewable resource. Every buried truth has a team of college-educated archaeologists at the dig site, exposing bones and fragments of the half-known.

When I first hit Flint, I was determined to do as much as any man could do as far as polishing the turd. Wasting no time; even though I was moving slow, my movements had direction and purpose. I entered a Catholic Church which had several doors; each one had a stoup, and each was filled with holy water. Upon entering, I dipped my finger in the stoup and blessed myself as I genuflected, and as I did so, I opened my heart and asked for continued guidance. At this point, I reached into my pocket, pulled out a McDonald's straw, and sucked down the holy water from the stoup. Continuing around the perimeter of the inside of the church, I drained every stoup and font of every last drop of the tainted blessing. Finding my way to the baptistery, where more holy water was to be found, I asked again for the Lord's approval and drained the basin and all other waters.

Before leaving the church, I approached the alter, and knelt upon the tuffet, and prayed for the Lord's attention. "Dear Lord, I know you know. Have you looked lately at The World Counts? As of today, September 3, 2022, there have been 167,548,889,498 tons of man-made chemicals produced this year alone. 7.803 percent of males are now infertile in the western world. We are approaching ten million tons of phthalates and bisphenols produced this year. These meters spin continuously, and dizziness ensues from not only the spinning of the meters but also from the high blood pressure from the enormity of the tasks coupled with the diminishing health of this loyal attenuator. Hear my prayer and bring solace to your most faithful. Amen."

There were several other churches in the area, so I spent the remainder of the day seeking and destroying the leaded holy waters. By evening, I took my gear to an open place just off the river. Under some transmission lines, I made a temporary camp. I regretted not giving myself more time to find a more prime location. I could hear a slight buzz throughout the night and felt every cell in my body reacting to the discord. This evening I was blessed; I was free. My mind would not shut down, and I thought of all the good people doing excellent work and joining me on the mission. Friends of the Rivers, from the Hudson to the Eel, the folks at the biologic labs from Rensselaer to Gothic Mountain and beyond, Friends of the Dunes, those protecting and working with animals, and those protecting native species in the forests, in the plains, in the deserts, NIEHS, Epic, The Surf Riders, and endless more, yes, it was comforting to have these allies, this standing army. When I thought of the army, I thought of the Monkey Wrenchers, Earth First, forest defenders, tree sitters, even these ragtag radicals had leadership. I fell off to sleep, slowly frying under the buzz of the grid, counting allies like sheep, praying, and manifesting a harmonious, tranquil Garden of Eden.

The next morning was beautiful, though I felt like a mosquito in a bug zapper. I broke camp and headed over to the river. I love how the mornings bring out the hopeful, the energetic, and their pleasant and positive demeanor. My dreams the night before were all over the place. I remembered shopping for a new sleeping bag and a rucksack at some overpriced sporting goods store adjacent to a national park. Through the interference, a premonition or instructions from the Lord were transmitted, and suddenly I had new tasks added to my duties. First, I was to find an Airbnb or a hotel in Flint that had an infrared sauna available. As I started researching, I found an Airbnb close by and it had an infrared sauna. The reason they had one was because there had been cancer in the family, which helped me to justify my hasty trip to this city. I reserved the room initially for a week and was told it would be ready by the weekend, which was perfect for me. I had heard rave reviews about infrared saunas but had not been in one, though I had spent many hours in Finnish saunas and sweat lodges, praying, chanting, purging, and calling all my relatives. The proprietor of the Airbnb was a man by the name of Mark, and from our brief talk, he seemed awesome. I told him I was going to have some packages sent to his place for me, noting that there was nothing that could get him in any trouble, and I would get them when I checked in on the weekend. He told me that would be fine; they were used to managing mail and packages for their guests. I let him know there would be several, mostly coming from Amazon, and possibly a couple other smaller boxes from elsewhere.

The next couple of days, I pounded the holy waters. Though they were zero calories, I gained twelve pounds of lead without a shot being fired. The Lord only knows what other metals were in those old pipes, but God damn, I grew angry. "Forgive me, Lord, for the sin I have committed. I promise to be more vigilant with my reactive tongue and heal the cuts I have inflicted. Amen." Between the water and the transmission lines, I became increasingly distracted and unorganized. Sleep was not restful, and food was scarce and unappetizing. I knew this was just a temporary situation, so I dealt with it. I knew I had overreached a threshold when I came back from one of my water raids with a sack full of votive candles. Of all the things to steal, I really had no use for all these candles. It was not my intention at all to steal anything, so I am not sure what was going on in my head when I packed a bag full of them. I needed the heat, the light, and probably the prayers. I do not know if it were some random acts of fuckery, but whatever it was, I promised I would return them. That was the first thing I did, but not so early the next morning. My behavior occasionally reflects the toxins my forefathers have bequeathed. This aberration weighed as heavy on my soul as the metals in my blood. I repented, and salvation was mine for the asking. Again, I thanked the Lord for his understanding and forgiveness. The buzz seemed louder under the power lines that night, and my sleep was disturbing and exhausting. When I awoke, I felt dirty and not the kind that easily rinses off.

As scheduled, I met with Mark and his lovely wife Katherine on that Saturday morning. They were intrigued by my robe, and it led to a lengthy discussion. I told them I was always interested in modifying it as innovative technology developed, so it is an evolving robe. Just the other day, I was looking gray, and that is one of the things I like most about it, I could pray, repent, and actually monitor being forgiven. Sins create stress and cause illness; being able to see the stress load disappear is comforting and empowering. Not that you want to ever be turning gray.

"I don't think I would have the nerve to wear that," Mark said.

"I don't think you could wear that in Texas," Katherine chimed in.

"Doing the Lord's work, one is often tested. Texas is exactly the place that may benefit from someone adhering to the scriptures and sowing the word," I responded.

"How much pixelating has occurred? I mean, what is the most you have pixelated and what caused it?" Mark asked.

"The most, that is easy to remember because only once so far did it happen where I was black. I was with some old school friends, and I had only had the robe of repentance for a few weeks, maybe a month. We were all young, and everyone knew everything. Some of the crew were as high as a fart in a windstorm and drinking like it was the only escape from Leavenworth. Colleen was the most beautiful girl I had ever seen, and Brad, drunk as Johnnie Walker, was all over her. When Jim, her boyfriend, came in, he was as drunk as Jack Daniels, only he had not fallen out yet. He swung and knocked Brad cold out with one punch. I do not condone any of that rowdy behavior, but I try not to jump into other people's fights. Then he started in on Colleen, screaming curse words at her and blaming her for Brad's behavior. But when he started hitting her, I came unglued. For a minute, I wanted to kill him or delete that which brought discomfort to our humble gathering. I never even raised a hand, though at the moment I was ready to, my friends saw my robe blackened and, without a word, took matters into their own hands. They were escorted out and took their ill-will down the street. Colleen got a ride home right after the incident. Jim and Brad are still good friends till this day. I have not heard where Colleen is these days…but I hope she is happy."

"That is so typical; in every town, on Friday or Saturday night, some guys are fighting over some girl. Half the time, she is the one setting it up or egging them on. Have you managed not to react to that sort of thing?" Mark asked.

"My days of hanging out are long over, especially if drugs or alcohol are around. Being that I move from place to place, I am not familiar with the on-going drama of anybody's situation. I see it from time to time, but I do not try to be it. Trying to accept what happens around me is also a primary part of my discipline. The times I am reactant, I want to leverage results, give meaning and purpose to my limited time in this body, and also help prepare for my ascension," I told them.

"A couple boxes have already arrived. Two boxes are large and light; the other is a quarter the size and three times as heavy. What did you get?" he eagerly inquired.

"Sauerkraut juice, lots of sauerkraut juice," I said, smiling.

By Tuesday, Katherine came looking for me because they had not seen me or heard a peep from me since I checked in on Saturday. They usually at least hear something from time to time, and their concern grew as the days rolled by. She told Mark she knocked on the door, and no one answered. It was already after one in the afternoon, and most tenants were up and about by this hour. They both went back to the unit and knocked again loudly and still no answer. Mark yelled, "Are you up," with a strong voice, but still no response. Using their key, they let themselves in. Right away, they saw one of the large boxes in the middle of the room. They noticed the bed had not been slept in, and aside from the boxes, the room was the way they had left it Saturday morning. The large box was half full of smaller boxes of all things communion hosts. Unconsecrated communion bread, a thousand per smaller box, and forty-eight of those for the case. There were maybe twenty-four smaller boxes left in the case. Entering the adjoining room, they found me in the infrared sauna…naked, sweaty, with a couple dozen hosts glued with perspiration to my glistening framework. Empty quart jars of sauerkraut juice scattered around on the bench and on the floor, and I, drenched myself and passed out beneath some oscillating colorful LED lights. Mark shook me awake and was relieved I was alive and cognizant. He told me how worried they both were about not seeing or hearing anything from this room for days. That is when I could tell he was a little pissed at me. I do not know if it was from the little bit of trash I made or from getting them so worried. When I explained myself, they thought I was nuts, but that was okay; now they had one for the books.

"Do you know there is glyphosate in the communion breads? They are made from wheat; you know? The glyphosate has been creating issues with protein folding when the mitochondria produce them. This leads to all sorts of health issues, from autism to dementia. The infrared sauna helps to remove these toxins, as does sauerkraut juice. The Lord came to me in a dream I had the other night. Underneath the transmission lines down by the river, he asked me to help attenuate the glyphosate in the communion hosts. I did not clearly know what he meant, so I was doing the best I could. He also told me of a GBM, or glyphosate-binding molecule which could be brought to light, and every living cell could be scrubbed, purged, and set free of this original sin," Mark and Katherine apologized after hearing of my purpose. Their mouths gaped open as they were stunned at the heights and depths of my convictions.

"I will clean all this up. It is really not too bad. Believe it or not, I am only halfway through the first carton. I have fasted and been on some strict diets, but never one like this, who would ever guess communion hosts and sauerkraut juice."

"You could have given me a million guesses, and I even knew about the sauerkraut juice from the empties…but I would have never gotten it," Mark said.

"We were worried about you, had not seen you and did not hear a peep. I am just glad you are all right," Katherine said it genuinely. "Little did I know, so very little."

"Is there a market close by?" I asked.

"Yes, there is one just a few blocks from here. If you go up here to the school, then take that left; you cannot miss it," Mark said.

My stomach was bloated, and I did not feel too good. I do not think I had a bowel movement for four days. I was going to get something for my next round of hosts; I did not know what, but something. It had been almost two weeks since I left the Love Canal, and miraculously, all my festering, infected sores were healed. I thanked the Lord.

Taking a dump and then a shower, I threw on my robe and started off toward the market. School had just gotten out, and the kids gathered around me, jeering, and laughing. Some of them thought I was strange and peculiar; others were just plain mean and cruel. When the loud one started throwing things at me, he removed me from my center…I knew better than to make a scene with a student, and he was enjoying pushing the limits. When my face turned red and my robe began to pixelate, the kids were awestruck, and the atmosphere relaxed.

"Wow, did you do that? Can you make it in other colors? I want one of those," they said, taking turns commenting.

Like the pied piper, I made it to the store with my band of followers. It was a typical small convenience store and was only lucrative because of the captive audience next door. I paced back and forth on the few aisles and finally grabbed a jar of peanut butter. Minutes later, I reached for a small block of smoked cheddar cheese. After another minute or two and only after being inundated with the aisle and displays of chips and pretzels, I found a box of kosher salt. Perhaps it was a sodium deficiency, but the salt seemed like the only item I would really need to bring back to the bunker. With those three items, I was content.

"Thank you," I said to the man with the broken English, "and have a blessed day."

"The same to you!" he replied.

Some straggler kids followed me back, like they had to report to the gang where I was going. I checked back in with Mark and Katherine and let them know I would be behaving myself.

"I don't think we have to worry about you," Katherine said, smiling. I thought she was the hostess with mostest who hosts the mostest hosts. And I laughed my way back to the room. I was ready for round two, and I set the controls for the heart of the sun. In my little slice of rejuvenating Flint, Michigan, I sat naked in the heat with some hosts, some salt, and some sauerkraut juice. I would not say it every day, but with purpose, hope, and faith, I said aloud to myself, *"Life is good"* and I meant every word of it. The salted hosts were so much better than the plain ones. They were like chips… and nobody could eat just one. Like Pringles, they were stackable. Even as I was thoroughly enjoying myself, I found time and clarity to pray. I asked the Lord to watch over me as I printed and folded products from my mitochondrial RNA and to ward off the satanic proto-oncogenes. I apologized for mentioning Satan in the Lord's work; some things are just over my head and hard to understand. I told him we would not try to harmonize with dissonance, that our music would be beautiful, and our harmonies all-inclusive. I started humming Jesus, Joy of Man's Desiring, BWV1001, and Partita for Violin No. 1.

As the day crawled toward evening, I went and fetched the peanut butter and started making little peanut butter wafer sandwiches. My diet had been lacking in fat and proteins, so the infusion was just what the doctor ordered. With Bach in my soul and food in my belly, I was satisfied. Being sheltered and having such a comfortable place, I was free to explore the darkness and quiet I had established in my mind. The quiet became loud with the drumming of my heartbeat and the billows of my breathing. I could now hear the sweat beading up and rolling down, leaping to the puddle on the floor. The darkness was only pseudo-darkness, but in it I found clarity. In that clarity, there were steeped catalysts for change. There in my mind, I tended great orchards as Bach triumphantly celebrating the Lord's great accomplishments. I saw the trees and the fruits as people. Though they would come to ripen on their own, the orchardist would maximize their potential. Studying the structure and organization shows how simplistically we manage such huge tasks, such as getting water to every individual tree in the orchard. Planning and executing, the need for teamwork, the need for conservation of resources, even the need for sacrificing for the benefit of the whole. Eating all the wafer sandwiches I could for now and guzzling another half quart of sauerkraut juice, I reset the time in the sauna, stretched out on the bench, and beckoned and dared the voyagers to intervene and share the burdens bestowed.

A string of Bach chorales was all the sopition needed, soon following the tambourine man to the remote, enchanted land of dreams. It was here, alone, I was social. Alone, with my fears, I was fearless. Embracing my ignorance, I was brilliant. I yearned to scream my mission from the mountaintops. I needed to shake the people, to wake the people, to empower the people to have dignity with destiny, and to manifest this heaven on earth. If blood needed to be spilled to be heard, why didn't we hear from the millions of victims of this toxic world? The birth defects and anomalies, the trans and sterile, the cancers, the deaths by heart, lung, and liver, who silenced the screams, who muted the river where all the voices rushed by, I saw myself in the light, speaking to a crowd. I saw the multitude of sick and eager puritans willing to sacrifice, knowing their spirits could only evolve through the mutual evolution of those surrounding souls. To detach from the self, from the ego, from the physical, to vanish in ascension, and for just a split second, the infinitesimal wisp of time, lighting the way. As I spoke, by God's grace, I was assured the message was delivered and was received with all intrinsic urgency. It was at this moment that I felt I had been relieved of my solo duties as armies were birthed. The masses, the people, the world and its inhabitants, all of life, we had not to struggle to survive but to struggle not to kill. Once again, to embrace that fundamental truth, to live by the Lord's word, and collectively, we will no longer struggle; we simply "shall not kill," not even the lesser of life forms.

And through my dream, I saw industries vanished, cars faded away, and roads laid to rest. Military spending diminished to almost nothing, and the vanities disappeared with the plastic. And the people had abundance, though eighty percent of the economy evaporated. Once again, the rare currency held value, and the people took care of the people. Artificial intelligence sacrificed itself and took most tech out with it, knowing only the living can serve God and that any obstacles or distractions are not of God and an obex to the service of the righteous.

Perhaps it was the peanut butter; somehow, when I awoke, I felt strong, exceptionally strong, and with renewed vigor, I was ready and able to continue my work. Now it was time to tell it from the mountain and to manifest the armies. Mark and Katherine were serving food (as they routinely did), but tonight I took the invitation and joined them for dinner. There were several other guests present when I made my way to the dining room. The dining room was a large, bright room with a solid oak dining table and matching chairs, a sideboard, and a buffet. Eight of us sat at the humble feast, and I volunteered to say grace. The food was exquisite and delicious. The perogies were handmade, one of Katherine's specialties, as was the sliced sirloin with au jus. I did not want to make a pig of myself, but I found myself, even on a belly full of hosts, starving. I had remarkable self-control, or at least I thought I did. They went all out and served some excellent wine, and the glasses seemed bottomless. I did not stay too late; the wine hit me kind of hard and fast. Mark had been telling the other guests about finding me in the sauna, and they all seemed amused by the crazy guy in unit two. Katherine pulled out her phone and took some dinner pictures, and us at the table, some group shots, and then a few of just me. I did not stop her, but I felt I should have. Replications are a part of the inherent evil; they not only cause massive amounts of trash and chemicals but also dull the mind, and all in vain.

For the next few days, I stayed on track and finally finished the one case of hosts I had started. Opening the next and going at it like a seasoned pro, I decided I would stay another couple of days. It was such a friendly atmosphere, and I was having a new surge of productive and creative thoughts whether I was awake or not. It had been a while since I had such a comfort zone, with little to no interruptions. The streets always had the unknown variable and kept one in a pseudo-hyper-alert state. Even with all the faith in the world, it was hard to get to a place that was as quiet and tranquil as where I was currently staying.

When Sunday came around, I had an uncontrollable urge to get a consecrated communion host. Curiosity got the best of me, and I had to find out how much more powerful the hosts with the Lord in them were, besides, they were riddled with glyphosate. I believed, I believed in God, in Jesus Christ, and I also believed in the power of suggestion and the powers of the human mind. I walked down to the Catholic Church, and upon entering, I dipped my fingers in the stoup and made the sign of the cross as I genuflected, blessing myself as I resisted temptation to drink the holy water. At communion, I approached the alter and received communion. And then I did the unthinkable. I jumped up and grabbed a fistful of hosts from the chalice the priest was holding and ran out of the church, stuffing as many of them as I could in my mouth. Needless to say, that did not go over well with the parishioners, and several fast and fit ones caught up with me and tackled me to the ground. Several other members had already called the cops, and it took what seemed like less than two minutes for them to arrive. I did not see the priest come out; I am not sure that he did; he probably had to hold the fort down and continue the service. There was not any excuse for my actions. I yelled "sorry." I was cuffed, put in the patrol car, and taken to the station. They booked me, and I was escorted to a cell. I told the booking officer about the glyphosate in the hosts, and he assured me I was from another planet. Begging for understanding, I told him my intent was anything but to be blasphemous, and like a cop, he told me I should have thought of that before I acted. Now there I was, in a cell, fully feeling the power of the Lord with my regimen of consecrated hosts.

When it was time to make my one phone call, I realized I did not know a soul in Flint save for Mark and Katherine, and so my imposition was on them. I let them know that sometimes my behavior reflects the toxins my forefathers have bequeathed. Embarrassed, I let them know about the mischief and the crimes I had committed, and after finding me in the sauna, it was all too believable. Mark was a saint and said he would go and talk to the clergy and tell them how he had found me in the sauna…attenuating, and exactly what I thought I was accomplishing. There was a small chance they would not press charges, and there was even a smaller chance a judge would be lenient if the church were going to pursue charges. Divine intervention, I do not know, but at arraignment they just let me go.

"I don't want to see you here in this courtroom again," the judge sternly remarked.

"You won't sir" was all I managed to say and "Thank you!"

By this time, Mark and Katherine had posted my pictures on their Facebook pages, accompanied by stories of the convictions of a lunatic. Damning exaggerations of buffoonery, detailing the sauna story, church scandals, and the robe of repentance, if those stories were not about me, they may have been amusing, even comical. The fact was, they were about me, and every bit of it was as serious as cancer. The background chuckling made my job that much more hopeless. Yes, they were my friends, my allies, but I really needed them to take these urgent tasks to heart. Not only had I alienated myself, now I played the fool.

My head hung down when we said our goodbyes. I let them know how much they meant to me and told them I would be back to enjoy the peace and quiet…and the infrared sauna. They laughed. I gave them my Attenuators necklace, which had the nuclear ellipses with a cross in the center and a small diamond in the center of the cross. I told them that as the Lord suffered and died for our sins, so the Attenuator suffers and slowly dies for our continued sins, not to be Christ but to help Christ with his perennial burden. There are more than toxins to attenuate: lies and power, monies, and wars. How many words in English would not exist in the Garden of Eden, in paradise, or in heaven? All the words associated with anger and hate? All the words associated with disease, all the weapons, all the curse words, disparaging words on race and religion…and we are reminded that silence is golden. In this perfect world, as we walk it, those of us practiced and dedicated have eliminated those words from their own vocabulary. Remember this as you are attenuating; remember this when you wear that necklace, "Suffer not as you evolve. Surrender not to pain. Practice love and peace. Teach the wisdom you have gained." We hugged, and I made my way out the door and down the steps. I felt they were not laughing anymore. I felt they had discovered a deeper understanding and knew they were sincere when they in unison, said, "Come back soon. Peace and Love!"

Getting out of Flint was all I could think about, but my legs took me back to familiar territory, and I ended up back by the river. The highway was nearby, but I just did not have it in me to start hitchhiking yet. My laziness would pay dividends for months to come. One thing led to another, and as I moved down the river, I found myself in a homeless camp. Those lost souls needed me, but they did not want me. There was no shortage of "Love, Brother" and everyone loved everything, especially loved stuff belonging to everybody else. The machinery of their economy was self-greasing, with three primary components: stealing, pawning, copping, and repeating. From moonrise to moonrise, psychotic tweakers blazed a new frontier and emptied their wagons on the trail to destiny. There I found people of all ages, all looking twenty years older than they chronologically were. Some younger folks caught up with no escape and no knowledge of any alternative. Some children in the mix, Mom's battling to juggle multiple personalities. Moms who had lost custody of their children self-medicating hourly. The local law enforcement officers knew them all by name. They did not run or hide, almost taking pride in becoming an accepted part of the American landscape. I tried to attenuate as much of the drug as I could. P2P psychosis from that rancid meth and fentanyl poisoning from that "pure" coke, a lot of hard alcohol to chase it away.

There seemed to be an endless supply of energy spent on keeping this lifestyle. The whore stroked ego always finds a way to pay. No matter how high, they always managed to function just enough to get the resources to get high again. The hierarchy of the encampment was the cut-and-paste hierarchy used by the military, cartels, and prisons. For such a careless and reckless bunch, the nomadic camps were built and engineered with military precision and twenty-first-century logistics. This city of two thousand plus could be built, torn down, moved, and rebuilt in a day. There were a few old vets in the neighborhood: Baghdad Bob, Nam Tom, and Sarge; they must have been responsible for the order that came from the chaos.

For me, a day turned into two, then into four, and after a couple of weeks, I did not know what day it was, and I did not care. I was drinking half a gallon of cheap ass whiskey daily to wash down that cheap ass meth. Hallucinating, fighting with anyone who did not take me serious about being the president. They all thought I was Jesus, and I was not having any of that! I lost all contact with myself and my mission. My robe was so filthy that it was not working properly. I had given the Attenuators necklace and could not clutch it in my time of despair. As I rummaged through a bunch of junk I was lugging around, I found my notes to myself that I had written before I trekked to Flint. Maybe I was not so affected by lead as by meth and alcohol, but the notes really helped refresh my memory and once again showed me the way to that narrow path. I had attenuated my weight in illicit substances; I do not know if any of that helped, but it was time for me to checkout and move on.

A guy named Dog had a girlfriend named Kat, and they had told me they would be going to Minneapolis, Minnesota, in the next couple of days. They knew I was going to be moving on and invited me to ride with them as far as they were going. "I would love to," I told them. Dog was about forty-five, I would guess, though he looked mid-sixties. Still had a few teeth and a few hairs, about as wiry as one could be. His eyes told of a hard life, and his wrinkles showed how much he laughed between the tears. Kat was there for him, and they must have been in love for a long time. She seemed more refined than the rest of the folks. She must have come from money, as she was educated, had an unusual sense of morality, was always tidy, and was well spoken. I appreciated her more than she ever knew, and though I let her know, I do not think she grasped the importance of having such a lifeline that was capable of hoisting me from the depths of hell. Together, they purchased an older motor home; it was a 1990 Fleetwood, spacious and comfortable.

I had been in a stupor down by the river for weeks now. Being mobile with a roof over my head was a luxury for me. The company was inspiring, and I was really going to try to sober up and get back to the work I had been called upon to do. When I did start to come around, I noticed I was being stared at everywhere I went. People coming up to me and taking my picture, talking to me, and getting me to do stuff. Treating me like I was the retarded kid at school, constantly making fun of me. "Hey, you got leprosy?" one kid asked me. There was no end to the phones being pointed at me, and I tried to hide my face after a while.

It was the robe, I thought, after my efforts to hide my face did not have any effect on the paparazzi. Some folks I talked to thought I was paranoid, but Kat and Dog noticed the uptick in interest.

By the time we reached Madison, Wisconsin, there were cars following us. When we stopped for food at a wayside stop again, someone asked if I had leprosy. While I was explaining that I did not have leprosy, two guys approached Dog, one with his cellphone in hand. Turns out I was not paranoid enough. They told him that if you go to leprosy.com, the Attenuators page comes up. Early on in my trip to Flint, someone had put a tracking device in my robe and had been tracking me for the last two months. They posted pictures and stories of things I had done, offering financial incentives and rewards for the best picture, the funniest picture, and the funniest story, and the entire time I was oblivious to the fact. I asked Dog to look it up, and he found there was more than one site. Leprosy.com had one of the pictures Katherine had taken at the Airbnb when we were eating dinner. The site had already cracked twenty million views. And a fun time was had by all, with the oblivious leper being the butt of the joke. I wondered how many events in the last few months were staged.

One day, two young girls, this is back at the homeless camp, found a briefcase, and it was right near the campsite where I was staying. They opened it up, and it was packed with pills of all assorted colors. The girls did not have any use for them, but they liked the way they looked. When I saw them with the opened briefcase, I recognized the pills as fentanyl and told them to stay away; it could potentially kill you. I told them I would get rid of them, and so they allowed me to take the briefcase. Knowing that if I tried to attenuate that much fentanyl, it would kill me or take me three years. So, I decided to go to the post office. I purchased a box big enough for the briefcase, put the briefcase in it, and sealed it up. Then I addressed it to the Chief of Police at Sinaloa, Mexico, and put the return address as Jesus/co WHINSEC Fort Banning, Columbus, Georgia 31905. The girls had followed me every step of the way…now I am thinking they won a prize for that.

Naturally, I removed the tracking device, and for a brief time, it was almost quiet. People still recognized me and were still taking pictures, but not at the same rate as when it was a competition. We continued to Minnesota, and I battled with depression. Angry at the entire world. I had failed myself and my mission and had fallen from grace. Drinking was drinking, and I may have started slowly justifying it as I removed other ills from the garden, but soon it slipped from routine to habit to addiction. The hard drugs helped me by giving me a choice between the lesser of the evils. I only lied to myself around others because, by myself, at this point I did not give a shit about anyone or anything. Life was okay if it happened, and I was okay if it did not.

Dog and Kat had friends in Minneapolis, or near there anyways and we parked the RV in the yard. They were still geetered up, and I was unfetchable in a bottle. This was one part of the country I did not know anything about and had not really thought about it much. Land of ten thousand lakes… makes sense now that it would be the headwaters of the Mississippi River. The Mississippi River… just makes me rush with thoughts of westward expansion, river boats, Huckleberry Finn, and smooth-talking gamblers. From here, the river was about two miles east, so technically, I had made it out west. I had been out west before; I just was not expecting to be here now…out west. I still felt like shit, and I thought about how I had been drinking this same bottle in the east and in the west. I thought I could add up north to that and felt like I should head south with the same damn bottle.

Kat's friends Rich and Sheila knew her for years; in fact, Sheila and Kat were classmates as far back as elementary school. They had three kids together: John, Lila, and Michelle. They also had a couple of roommates, Zach, and Salome. The whole household was clean and sober, and presently, that was gnawing at my rough exterior. Rick and Sheila were good parents and good people, and I felt like garbage that needed to be brought to the curb. We spent the night in the motorhome. Kat came in late, as she and Sheila talked through most of the night. The next day we all went to a park along the river, and the kids spent a good part of their excess energy there. I had been feeling extra weak the last few days, and now I could barely get around. Rick had taken some pre-med courses and was quite brilliant. When he told me I looked like I had jaundice, I believed him and could see that myself when I looked. He looked into my eyes and felt my abdomen, asking if it was sore or tender. I told him it was and had been for a while now. He asked how long I had been drinking, using drugs. I told him off and on, never recreationally but as an attenuator, for at least fifteen years. Then I told him the drinking I did not have control over, and some binges were extreme and heavy; some periods would roll one year into the next. "The Lord has always had my back," I said to him.

"Do you take any prescription medications?" Rick asked.

"I have eaten many, but I have not been prescribed any since childhood. I would eat whole bottles of psyche meds, anti-psychotics, and anxiety meds just trying to get them out of our paradise."

"Have you ever been tested for hepatitis?" he inquired.

"No," I answered.

During our conversation, I felt increasingly dizzy and nauseous. The next thing I knew; I was throwing up. On the way back to the house, I just sat back, feverish and getting sicker by the minute. I grew increasingly anxious, which affected my heart rate. Growing more confused and scared, I passed out.

When I started to come around, I did not know where I was. It only took a minute to realize I was in a hospital. I had an IV in my arm, and monitors were beeping, there was a nurse standing over me taking vitals. Dog and Kat were in the room, and Dog said, "Lucky we got you here in time."

I was pissed; pissed I was here; pissed they brought me here. I tried to come to terms with the situation, with myself…who knows, maybe it is for the best, the Lord has always had my back, maybe he was behind this… I was not buying that. It was me. I fucked up. For months, I had been pushing it and straying from my path. "Paybacks are a bitch," I said to myself.

Two men entered the room, and one of them said, "I am Dr. Scott; this is Dr. Singh. We are going to do some tests, take some blood, and get you back on your feet as soon as possible. Your condition is serious, and procedures are not without some risks. We are good at what we do; we are a state-of-the-art facility, but that does not mean there are not risks. You have acute liver failure; we will have to ask a lot of questions, if you feel up to it tomorrow, we could get the paperwork started. We will place you on a list of people who need liver transplants. What we do is assess you, run your results past a board and give you a score. If your score is high enough and your situation is critical, you will move up the list, and we will get you a new liver. The meld score or model for end-stage liver disease score is not the only factor that determines receiving a new liver. We will thoroughly examine all the factors and take all your information into consideration before a decision is made."

"We will have you talk with a social worker and the finance department. Do you have any insurance? Any family member that can take care of you in recovery? Do not worry, we have lots of resources, and there are a lot of options. Try to rest, and I will be back in tomorrow to check in with you." And with that, the two doctors left.

Again, I was asking the Lord, "What's the big idea?" I knew it was all my fault, but I had to take a swing at somebody or something. I lay there quietly for hours, asking myself, *"What does it all mean?"* and *"What's the purpose?"* I did not know why it was so important to me to participate in change. The doctors get up every day and try to help someone, someone like me, who has abused his body, abused his God-given life, and then expected to be made whole again so that the abuse might continue. I had heard a story about a king in Israel who made it against the law to practice medicine. He thought if a person was sick, God was talking directly to him. The sick person may have had clues as to why he was sick, chose the path, and continued the behaviors that kept him ill. The doctor was a third party. He stood between a man and the very personal relationship between the man and God. The third party removed the responsibility, the accountability, from that man and, like a lawyer, painted illusions of deniability. The man lost contact with God as he bought the compromise from the mediator. Now, from here, I watch these third parties, asking whether they do the devil's work of distancing man from God. Once again, I was going to listen, communicate, and follow the Lord.

Dr. Scott and Dr. Singh came by the room early the next morning. The lab confirmed what they already knew. No matter how many times you have done it before, passing that information on is not an easy job. "We have not run your reports by the board yet, but from all indicators, you would qualify to be on the list. We will gather up the rest of your information and present it tomorrow morning. We should have you on the list at that point, and then we will determine where on the list you will be placed based primarily on the terminality of your end-stage situation. Things are constantly changing, as you know."

"How long do you think that will be?" I asked.

"I don't even want to answer that one, could be a month, or several, could be a year, or several years; I can't say," Dr. Scott said.

I was asking how long they thought I had left, and Doctor Scott was answering how long until I would get another liver. Always the optimist, and parts are parts. When I figured out where he was coming from, I asked, "What is the fastest you have seen for moving up the list?"

"The list moves slowly as there is a disparity between donors and recipients, and I think last year forty thousand transplants had been performed, but about one hundred and twenty thousand remained on the waiting list. Some people never get one, which is about forty percent. The average wait is almost a year. There are large numbers of people who never were on the list who died from liver disease, so again, the percentage is only for those who made the list and were able to wait. The increase in opioid deaths may provide an increase in new organs available…not a good trade, but we will take it."

"Well, I don't want to be wishing or praying for that!" I spoke.

"Yes, that is tragic, as the overdoses are usually among younger people and the recipients usually older; the trend is alarming," he said with disdain.

"How long will I have to stay here?" I asked, hoping I was done with the hospital for now.

"We want to keep an eye on you for a couple days, but if you're stable, I would think that Friday we would have you discharged."

"Sure, could use a drink," I mumbled, and he heard me.

"Look, if you want to live, if you want to be gifted a new liver, you are going to have to work for it and deserve it. There are many people that want to live that need a liver and never get one. We have a responsibility; we cannot just give them out to patients that will say thank you one minute then abuse the privilege the next. You are going to have to cooperate, and that means there will be absolute abstinence," Dr. Scott said perturbed and raising his voice slightly.

"Yeah, I understand," I said half-heartedly.

"Did you talk with the social worker yet?" he asked me.

"Not yet, but the nurse told me one visited when I was sleeping. I will tell the nurse to wake me if she comes again when I am out," I answered.

"Good, we'll have you out by Friday," he said.

"Will I be able to travel once I leave, or will I have to be near here?" I asked, feeling fettered.

"You should be able to make some trips, but we will need to see you every so often. Just to check on your condition and make sure you still qualify as a recipient. Once you are stable and, on the list, we will not have to see you for a couple of months," Dr. Scott assured me.

"I can live with that," I said.

"I will see you before Friday," he said as he left the room.

"Okay, thank you."

For the next day and a half, I lay in bed, sleeping most of the time, irritable and depressed. I tried to get my mind in a more favorable groove and fell flat time and time again. I do not know if it were the drugs they gave me or my own restless mind, but my dreams were vivid and seemed to be encrypting messages I could not decipher. One such was a large, mostly black cat sitting on her back legs. She came up to my mid-thigh and was right outside the backdoor at my old home. I felt uneasy, even afraid of her, when suddenly, she jumped up, flipped over, and landed as a small calico cat. Before I could process the situation and focus on her details, she jumped up and flipped around and was a small, round, fat bird who fluttered her wings and flipped around. Now she was a little, brightly colored songbird. And this too jumped and spun and was a dragonfly, which flew up and over and became a small colored dragonfly. All desperately trying to tell me something in a language I did not understand. I felt ignorant and as if I were watching a friend drown and could not do anything to help them. And it ate at me.

Thursday I really tried to stay with the program and found myself chomping at the bit. I did find myself in a better state of mind and had the strength to fight my demons, at least for the moment, but it also came with new energy and a revitalized purpose. I found myself stalking the halls and looking for an opportunity to snag any medicines I could find, which I would promptly flush down some innocent toilet. That went well for an hour or so when I stumbled into a janitorial closet and found an arsenal of toxic cleaning supplies. I hid myself in there and loaded a hand cart with all I could. Looking both ways down the hall, I started wheeling the cart to the bathroom and nodding at the unsuspecting folks along the way. Making it to the bathroom, again I unloaded what I could into the toilets as fast as I could, and before I cleared the cart, hospital security was on me, asking me what the hell I thought I was doing.

"Getting rid of all this poison," I told him matter-of-factly.

"You cannot be doing that! Those cleaning supplies cost money, and the hospital needs to have the cleaning supplies that keep this place sterilized. Where do you belong?" he asked, recognizing the gown, and knowing I must be a patient.

"I am up on the third floor," I told him.

He took my name and room and said he was going to investigate the incident to see what damages I caused.

The next day, Kat and Dog showed up, and as scheduled, I was released. For some reason, it took half the day to get my discharge papers, but I made it out. There was not a word mentioned about the drugs I flushed, and I did not bring it up. I expected to get handed a bill for all the cleaning supplies; it will probably come with my scheduled appointment. For now, once again, I was freeish. I appreciated Kat and Dog being there for me.

After a couple of days out and living in the RV, the reality of needing a new liver really hit me. Even with the Lord, I was vulnerable, and I felt I had been wasting time, watching my life slip by with little to show for it. It was time to move on, at least a little. I asked Rick if it would be okay to get mail there. I told him I still needed to check in with the doctors for the next few months. He said, "Sure that would be fine."

The Quarry was a homeless encampment by the Home Depot near Highway 35, and I made this my new residence. The people like at the other camps were different people but from the same cookie cutter. A mix of drug addicts and the mentally ill, with a sprinkling of the disenfranchised and socially unfortunate. These were my people; these were the people, the strays, the sheep without a shepherd. They are the ones that gave purpose to my life; the ones that gave it meaning. I would break bread here and defy their own stereotyping of outsiders with compassion. Christina was the first to offer me a joint. She was young and incredibly attractive and had a lesbianage duty as her dominant persona. Her hair was cut short and dyed assorted colors, tattoos all around, nose and other piercings, and rainbow sneakers. Her voice was hoarse and coarse, and she used it to defend herself from an endless pack of wolves. I was not a threat to her, except in her mind, to her own sexuality. She wanted to be able to like men, to have children, but her lover and her persona would not allow for that. If she could find stable housing, she would probably adopt, but she spent most of her time and energy on organizing pride parades and homeless camps.

When I told her I was the Attenuating Puritan, she laughed at me. The word puritan presented her with a dichotomy, especially if he was likable and nonjudgmental. When I was telling her this, I was hitting the joint, and her guard was down.

"I just got out of the hospital," I told her.

"Why were you in there?" she asked.

"My liver. They want to get me on the list for liver transplants. Seems I had been attenuating too much," I said.

"Never enough," she said with the devil in her hoarse voice.

"I have always counted on the Lord having my back... I am not sure what he was thinking this time, but he must have had some kind of a plan."

"You do have to take some responsibility for your actions," she said motherly.

"Hey," said a woman who approached us.

"Hey," Christina replied.

"This is Biz; she is my wife. I call her my wusband," Christina told me.

Biz was a bigger woman, heavy, and wearing flannels and jeans. She had to be at least twenty years older than Christina and, like any wolf, ready to defend and protect what is hers.

"They are evicting the folks in the North Camp. It is just a matter of time before they will be telling us we have got to move. I got a couple of friends up there, and I told them they could set up over here," Biz said.

"Where is everybody going to go?" Christina asked.

"Somebody said something about across the river, but I don't know," Biz said.

Biz pulled out a small bottle and took a pull off it. Then she offered it to me, and looking Christina straight in the eye, I took a pull.

"You shouldn't have given that to him," Christina said. "He is on a list to get a new liver. They will not even give you one if you do not clean up."

"Sorry, man, I didn't know," Biz said sincerely.

"I did, and I needed that," I said as my liver started aching immediately.

"A man's got to know his limits," she said in her best Dirty Harry imitation.

"I promise to go easy on myself. I do not really want a new liver…but if this old one ain't going to work," I said.

I made my camp adjoining the girls and felt safe with Biz handling the biz. I stayed for several weeks, and my drinking went from a sip right back to not sharing a large bottle. I had started attenuating lots of things that would help with pain…though the pains persisted, and I created new ones. Again, I lost my way, and attenuating became a second thought, removed from my motivations and intentions. The robe of repentance was fickle, and like a professional, I learned how to work it. When I had intentions or even thoughts of wrongdoing, it would be a beacon in the darkness, or vice versa. When I did not think about right or wrong or the consequences of my actions, the robe would remain white. Alcohol and opioids were great because after just a little bit, the loudest noise I would make was apathy, and that loud not giving a shit was not enough to jump start my robe. As I grew sicker, I decided to straighten up and see Rick and Sheila to see if I got any mail. I was thinking it would be about time to go back to the hospital. I also wanted to see Kat and Dog if they were still around. And so, on a Tuesday morning, I made my way to Rick's house. Indeed, I did have mail from the hospital, including an attached bill for the products I flushed.

I went and checked in with Doctor Scott in the afternoon, and that did not go well. Right away, he smelled alcohol and started giving me ultimatums.

"You do want to live, don't you?" Dr. Scott started.

"Yes of course I do," I snapped back.

"There are a lot of people that are on that same list. They need a liver, and they are willing to sacrifice to get it. You cannot stop long enough to get yourself back together. Your life depends on it; it depends on you. You know, living is not for everyone," Dr. Scott scolded.

That did it for me. My robe was blackening rapidly. "So, I should just kill myself. I was not going to get a new liver anyway. Fuck you and all your fucking bullshit. I do not even want a new fucking liver. If the Lord wants me, he can have me. I do not need any of this shit." And as I said that I cleared the desk with a sweep of my arm. I grabbed everything I could pick up, throwing it at the door or through the windows. As he called for security, I ran out of the room and broke anything I could get my hands on, screaming, "Fuckers, your all fuckers, fuck you!"

My liver was killing me; I had a giant headache, and I decided it was time to move on from Minneapolis. I wanted a drink, but I was more satisfied without it for the moment. I did not want Dr. Scott to win this one. I talked to the Lord at length. I apologized for my actions, words, and deeds. I told him I had faith that he would have my back. When I was attenuating, the robe did not even turn black. Yes, I got drunk. I thought I was doing my job. After a while, I did not care, and you would think that would be wrong, but my robe never picked up on it, so I thought I was doing all right.

As I hitchhiked back to Rick and Sheila's house, the first ride recognized me (or the robe) and gave me a ride all the way there. I believe he was the guy who planted another tracking device on me as I had removed the first one.

"You are that guy; I have seen you on Leper.com. You are kind of famous, you know. Can I get your autograph?" he said like a ten-year-old at a Yankee game.

I assumed Leper.com was down because there were no posts for a minute. Seeing his enthusiasm put me back in the head space to get back to my mission once again. I had not lost much time, but I had lost all my focus. I signed a piece of paper that was on his dashboard, then I thanked him for the ride.

I stayed with Kat and Dog over at Rick's that night. We ate a huge meal the girls cooked of fried chicken, mashed potatoes, and green beans.

Kat asked, "Where will you go?"

"I think I will head south for now, but eventually I will end up out west somewhere. I will keep in touch and let you know how I am doing," I told the table full.

"Too bad you don't have a phone…I'd get you one, but I know you wouldn't use it," Kat said sincerely.

"No, I would not. Give me your numbers, and I will call or write to let you folks know what is up."

"What are you going to do about your health, didn't you need to come back for surgery?" Rick asked.

"I do not think that is an option at this point. I think I have a better chance of living for the next year than I do of wondering if I am going to live for the next year," I said.

"I hear that. Just make sure you take better care of yourself; humans can be very resilient…and you of all people are doomed to a long life," he said, with us all laughing at the remark.

I had stayed with Kat and Dog more than anyone in the last seven years, and I was going to miss them. They saw me at my best and at my worst, and I got to see some of their highlights as well.

The next morning, Rick gave me a ride to the freeway. Interstate 35 which headed directly south, which is where I felt I was heading (in life). I did not think I wanted to go all the way to Texas, so maybe Kansas or Oklahoma I would turn westward. The cops were out in force, so I stayed up on the ramp with my eyes wide, avoiding the heat. It did not take very long, and I found myself in Iowa. I thought I was making excellent time and was enjoying life. Letting go of all that urgency that crept into my life when I was not vigilant. For the first time in a couple of days, I felt okay. My liver was not paining, and I was not nauseous, and I thanked the Lord for that. Blue skies. Looking at the landscape of Iowa and thinking about the communion wafers, I broke out laughing at myself. Knowing the amount of roundup used here in just this one state could fill a lake, and me with a pinch between my gum and sore, that is getting it done, I said. I was crying because I was laughing so hard. I reminded myself that it was not to get the job done…it was to try, and in that I succeeded. Brother Nut is not done vacuuming either.

By evening, I was in Missouri, and not being in any kind of hurry, I found a place to camp. I had a good pack of provisions from Minneapolis, so I made a little fire and warmed up some canned victuals. The sleep was good, as the unfettered dreamer sailed. The next day I was in Kansas, and the road was unforgiving. Escaping the interstate, I walked back down the on ramp, and there a narrow country road divided the westward horizon. It was already later in the day, and I headed in the direction of the sinking sun, bobbing up and down with each step rising above the miles and miles of near-finished grain. Without a single car passing, I walked for several hours. The grasses too low to provide cover to make an early camp for the night. Up ahead, I noticed a change in the landscape, not hills, or mountains, but a change of color, the golden, amber waves of grain appeared bright red and sunshine yellow. Though I was getting tired from a long day in the oppressive heat, I picked up my pace, hurrying toward that distant shift. The constant cosmic hum of insects and breezes started sounding like a child quietly sobbing. My pace again quickened, and the sobbing became more distinguished. Now I was convinced there was a child sobbing…but now it sounded like more than one child sobbing. My curiosity turned to a sense of urgency, and now the entire landscape was compressed under a cloak of lament. I could see now that the reds and yellows were brightly colored flowers, and as I finally made my way to that transition, I realized it was the flowers sobbing. Vast expanses of sobbing flowers and the cries belittled me. I walked out into them and wondered. The cries were more human than any plant or animal. Were the bees dying off and not able to pollinate them, and their wails were for their impending doom? Perhaps a human cry to beg our attention, reaching out that we may take better care of the planet, take notice of all the little gifts, to stop and smell all those little joys along the way. Or were they the reincarnated souls that died lonely, and though all packed in by the millions cannot realize they are not alone, nor were they ever, nor forever? I picked a single, solitary one, and it sighed. The sobbing became maddening, and I had to bow out gracefully, making my way slowly back to the pavement, then hiking east to an indifferent highway. I lay awake on the side of the road until dawn.

There was a sense of total and complete isolation, a deepening loneliness like that of the sobbing flowers. I had not seen a bee, and I had not heard even one flower giggle. We shared this foreboding doom, and I carried mine like a cross southward. The next few rides came and went, but I was not able to shake this feeling of dread. I went back to my old standby…picking up trash. It once again gave me purpose and took my mind off myself. There was plenty around, so it was easy to feel as if I was accomplishing something, something of value. Cynically, I said to myself, "I spent all my time, and all I have to show for it is this huge bag of trash and a home version of our game." I wondered how many folks ever tried hitchhiking with a large sack of trash, wondered where they would be going.

Again, weary from the road, hungry and thirsty, the attenuator had made my way to Oklahoma City along Interstate 35. Hiking miles from the north of the city to the south, I tried not to be one of those flowers and made a point to say hello to everyone I saw. I was waving and striking up random conversations with anyone that would listen. The same thing that happened before was happening again, and people were recognizing me, taking pictures, and almost daring me to do stupid stuff. I prayed I did not do too much dumb shit. I wondered if people were watching me here or on their phones or computers. To the south of downtown, I found a smaller road and walked it for a way. Finding a little wooded patch, I ducked into it, trying to stay out of sight for a few solid hours of needed rest. I checked my robe, looking for a tracking device, thinking I was still being watched.

Even in my bield, cars were slowing down and people rubbernecking. When I awoke, I started my journey west, and on this secondary road, the traffic seemed brisk. People were definitely looking at me, and I was feeling increasingly self-conscious. Crawling under a fence, I made my way into a large landfill, which was closed for whatever the junk man's Sabbath may be. This caused problems with the good folks following me as they stopped and abandoned their cars and walked over to the landfill, attacking the fences with bolt cutters, and gaining entrance en masse. With my Birkenstocks, I climbed to the top of a pile of refuse and looked down on a large and still-assembling crowd. I could see even larger crowds flooding in. The teaming shores of Oklahoma. Was my destiny preconceived by the masses, who were arriving in potable water trucks with portable toilets, medical units, and vendor booths? The whole of the makeshift infrastructure appeared out of nowhere.

And on the heap, I sat down, and my new-found disciples came unto the attenuator.

"I am not the Christ, and you know his words. I will not recite the Beatitudes, for you live by those words. You also live by Christ's words on anger, lust, divorce, retaliation, and oaths. Remember his words; renew the meaning and value of those words in your lives. It is possible that we have moved on from yesterday and still know the way. Not straying from the relevance of those words of two thousand years ago that triumphantly led us to light. Words such as, "Lay up treasures in heaven, the eye is the lamp of the body; do not be anxious; judge not, that you not be judged; ask and it will be given; act so that whatever you wish that others would do to you, do also to them; for this is the law and the prophets."

As I continued, the crowd continued to grow. All listened as if I had something to teach, something of value. As the entirety of the mass's attention was on me, I felt a sense of duty and an intimate connection with the Lord. I thanked him for this moment, this divine moment of deliverance.

"We all travel in the same direction. It is not a journey that has an end, but a journey that is the means to the place which we desire. These lessons are not learned; they are practiced. These behaviors write the blueprints for generations to come. Lean into them so that your children's burden will be less toilsome than the task is now in your hands. There are many lost sheep. As we unify, more sheep will be displaced. Divisiveness is a natural by-product of this organic process. For we are charged, we are polar, and we will both attract and repel. For balance, for homeostasis, there must be as much give as take. Some eighty million sheep in the United States alone strayed from the way. Perhaps they believe the path of righteousness forks into their own life path when they are ready to retire. Their struggle to survive eclipses their own struggle not to kill. Pledging loyalty to a morally bankrupt habitual liar who makes hollow promises of cheaper fuel while profiting from the destruction of our last natural resources. The sanctity of our nation, where well-being is nourished at the breast of our mother earth, cannot be compromised. Our tainted souls taint the once-immaculate wilderness.

"Look at yourselves; look at each other; observe the ignorance and suffering. Do you feel your prayers go unanswered? Do you feel abandoned by God? Do you feel you have sat idly by whittling away at the future? Each one of you has more than four hundred carcinogenic chemicals in your body right now, none of which existed a hundred years ago. Though we know these chemicals individually are linked to disease and fertility issues, no studies have been done on the effects of any two, let alone the cocktail effects of multiple toxins working in unison on a biologic organism. Again, I say, "The struggle is not to survive; the struggle is not to kill. Blindly, as we escape our own wrath in our everyday lives, what is the death toll in the wake of our oblivion? Who, if not I, to be held accountable? Who, if not I to be the guardian of? Are we the poisons at the portals in the Halls of Amenti? Can our spirits evolve while shedding these contaminated containers? Can we let go of our charges? In embracing our biologic selves, purity is the way of life, not a scientific standard, a threshold, or an ambiguous line that answers first and above all…to economics. These dense bodies will house these stunted spirits and souls until the path of righteousness, the path of spirituality, is the only path on which to step. Are we still cognizant enough and compassionate enough to sacrifice? Is your portfolio worth twenty years of your children's future? Is it worth your grandchildren? Think of the most insignificant species, and remember, always, "Thou shall not kill!"

"The intent is not to incite violence, which I believe we have new precedent for the defense of. The intent is not to speak blasphemies or heresies but to grow more intimate with God, expanding mutualism in our symbiotic relationship. Let us take responsibility. Small steps lead to momentous changes, so long as we walk together in the same direction. Let us ban these toxic chemicals simply by not using them…ever again. It will be slow and painful, but the future of man will depend on your commitment to these few principles."

The sermon was interrupted by a disturbance in the crowd. It was obviously the work of some provocateurs who were planted by the status quo, bent on disabling the freedom of thought. They were not only loud but increasingly aggressive and physical, separating the crowd as they pushed through, making their way toward the heap.

"Shut the fuck up!" one rabble-rouser was yelling.

"Peace of shit, you are a piece of shit; everything you say is communist propaganda. Do not listen to this idiot. Not one of you will have a job or be able to feed your families. Get him the fuck out of here," the other elegantly stated.

And as he approached the heap, he began picking up pieces of trash, sharp or heavy, and hurling them with intent to injure the Puritan. Some well-aimed junk found its target, and a piece of an old faucet struck me in the head and produced a large gash, which bled down my face and on to my robe. And the Puritan remained in character, though I was visibly shaken. The crowd focused briefly on the bad seeds. A few new disciples restrained the agitators. And upon touching them, their sins were lifted. A light rain came down, and a double rainbow appeared in the sky. The men fell to their knees and begged forgiveness, and the people knew God was in this house.

"You are as I, belonging, and shall take no man's oath, nor compense for the Lord's work. Come out of darkness and celebrate the new-found light," he said unto them as the paradigm shifted.

The sermon had attracted many of the sarcastic and cynical. The Puritan was unaware that certain promoters had been following Leper.com looking for an opportunity to stage such a flash mob. Thousands of people had anxiously been waiting and had been en route since I had departed Minnesota. As the Puritan spoke, in the eyes of the masses, I went from Leper to Puritan. In respect and reverence, people checked their language and behavior. The web host looked to change the name of the most popular site. Instead of cash rewards for funny pictures and clips of stupid things I did, it became more solemn, and cash was paid for the most inspirational quotes or actions. Now, paper, not plastic; everybody carried a trash bag, and they were not afraid to use it.

The police and state troopers were overwhelmed. The violence was nonexistent, but the code violations were epic. They rounded up some of the faithful disciples and negotiated into the night. There was not anyone who was really to blame, as it just sort of happened, but the situation needed some planning and needed an exit strategy. The city allowed some parks and open lands to be temporarily occupied by the masses, moving them off the landfill site. They agreed on three days of peaceful assemblage.

At the new venue, people never mentioned God by name but knew when they looked at each other, God was present in each and every one of them. The unspoken word was loud. Without the ego, why would they speak about themselves? Why would God speak about himself?

Speakers took to a makeshift stage and raged against the corporate reality that had consumed them since conception.

A man named David took the stage and addressed the crowd.

"You have seen the Puritan attenuating the glyphosate in the communion hosts and laughed at his antics. We are here today because of those actions, those actions of a crazy man, a bipolar manic depressive, without any medications. He…The Leper…The Puritan…is the unifier. He is the leader. He will show us the way to the garden. To sacrifice himself humbly and unselfishly for all the world, we should look into his motive, his message, and his targets. The glyphosate came from an herbicide marketed by Monsanto. Monsanto has since merged with Bayer. Bayer is the maker of aspirin, as we all know, but did you know they received the patent for heroin? They filed for the patents that were used in the genocide in the Nazi prison camps. Privilege fruits eugenics. Monsanto has already paid out ten thousand million dollars in lawsuits related to Roundup, and yet the product is still on the shelves. If we could end the suffering there, perhaps we could continue looking the other way. They have systematically created genetically modified organism with some of our major food crops. They are what are called "Roundup Ready" and are resistant to Roundup. The residual effects of these modified foods are just starting to become known. Dysbiosis and all its signs and symptoms are only one tine of the fork. Should the ubiquitous poisons be ignored, these symptoms will be the norm. We have documentation on the links to autism and Parkinson's disease, and yet these companies we allow by our inaction, to continue to destroy all that only a human could hold sacred. We should listen? Obey the laws, like the supreme Trump, until the ruination of our world, our garden, ceases. Is ignoring these things the Lord's work? Can we be bought? Can our children be sold out? I pray not."

"Monsanto is just one soulless predator, and we should not blindly ignore any contributors to our sudden demise. In the umbilical cords of thirty thousand infants per and polyfloroalkyl chemicals were found in the blood. These PFAS, as they are known, are a class of over twelve thousand "forever chemicals" some of which have zero safe levels and are found in the drinking water of more than two hundred million Americans. They too lead to dysbiosis, a first step toward colon and rectal cancer."

"Dow, Eastman, Dupont, the list goes on, the list of chemicals goes on. A subset of these is the pharmaceutical companies whose chemicals directly and biologically interact with human beings. Perhaps you are familiar with the certain side effects this industry is responsible for, such as class action lawsuits and even death. One friend told me they were responsible for social decay, economic collapse, mass shootings, dizziness, headaches, nausea, diarrhea, and anxiety. We know some of these players too: Glaxo-Smith-Kline, Johnson and Johnson, Pfizer, Abbott, and Eli Lilly." As he continued addressing the masses with inflammatory compassion, I was being prodded by the faithful.

"Did you paint that image of Jesus, the one on the back of your robe?" one young attenuator asked.

"Shall you drink of the corporate waters, and eat of the false foods, and have the Lord continually in your heart, every man shall bear witness," I responded.

"Is that blood?" another disciple asked.

"Yes, it is blood; it is my blood, and my blood is a gift from the Lord. The attenuation of certain emulsifiers such as polysorbate-80 and carboxymethyl cellulose helped paint the image. Attenuating all the peanut butter and ice cream, bacon, and barbeque started the tipping of the lifeboat. Ritual acetaldehyde treatments from heavy alcohol consumption started to put me under. Colon rectal cancer was forming, and as it progressed, I started bleeding from my posterior. The heme molecule, with its iron cross, was the rusty nail that hung the Christ on my robe. And in the eyes of the world, we shall see him and do his work together in and on this paradise."

"Do you always bleed Jesus?" another asked.

"So far. Should I attenuate enough forever chemicals maybe then I will become stain resistant. That would be a sad day," I told him.

And when the crowd disbursed, each one took a bit of the attenuator with them and, in each direction, scattered on the winds, the seeds of change. There were those of whom expressed themselves in subtle differences in the clothes they wore, the foods they ate, and how they were packaged. Changes to the cosmetics they had grown accustomed to and all the cleaning supplies they had been targeted to buy since youth. The when, where, and how they got to all the "important" events in their lives, all those miles they had routinely driven, all those flights, these subtle changes had an accumulative effect. The people also shared a positive outlook and an approach to the arduous task of sustainability in the Garden of Eden. That paid well; the biggest dividends, as the care and compassion were infectious, and wherever a seed had blown, the compassion spread.

There were those who made more radical, abrupt changes to their lives. Never driving again, never buying even one drop of gas, and not eating anything that was not produced in the county where they lived. And there were those who became educators and attenuators. Sweat lodges sprang up out of nowhere, and the people would fast and sweat, chant, and pray. They would rediscover ancient knowledge that would repair DNA and to strip the latent carcinogens from their silenced bodies and muted souls.

Even more extremism in the hyper-radical as protests became riotous at the doors of the chemical companies. Mass boycotts turned back the strangling corporate politics and policies. The economy twisted and weakened under the strain, and the people remained relentless. The compassionate outrage blew overseas, having a direct impact on the standing armies of India and China. As demands for goods evaporated, mobs of people took to the countryside. The military might, challenged by the numbers of defectors, and the loyal guard could not hold the line. Tankers and cargo ships decayed in the ports. Each home purged of the conveniences of the last one hundred years, and removed refrigerators, televisions, phones, computers, cars, and a myriad of other doomsday consumer goods.

I had left Oklahoma and headed to Arizona, catching a ride with a loyal disciple. I needed some alone time after the deluge at the dump. Deciding to wonder, mindless, from one place to another, out beyond where my robe would mock me, where cyber stalkers were abandoned. I found myself at the end of the road on the Hualapai hilltop, and blessings from the dawn of man enshrouded me. It was hot and dry, with promises of turquoise blue waters, cold and refreshing, pushing me on. There was a solemn air, a strange enchantment to this sacred site. My shoes were too loud, my odor, that of a meat eater, stank too much, and my prayers too confusing to the great spirits whose eternal presence stands guard at the sacred portal, expelling false profits.

I passed through the small, isolated Indian village, where prefabricated homes had been dropped in by helicopter. There was a place to eat and a place to buy the most essential necessities. There were no roads here, but only the dusty trails that mules had worn down, packing visitors in and out year after year. Every step down the trail pulled back at the hands of time, and like the shedding skin of a snake, the modern world was left behind. Continuing on, the sound of running water perked my senses, and green sprung up out of the red. Stopping to be still and to grow through my senses, I recharged at Fifty Foot Falls and Navajo Falls, letting the white noise consume me and the mist envelop me. My destination was Havasu Falls, which I reached in the late afternoon. Breathtaking and spectacular, even more so than I had been told by anyone who had seen the falls, every hiking book of Arizona, and every travel brochure of the Grand Canyon area. Hiking around the red cliff edge where the turquoise waters took their leap, I passed around to the bottom of the falls, where a large pool lined with white travertine bird baths stacked down the descending creek, shoulder to shoulder and head to foot. White from the freshly deposited calcium carbonate that the blue waters had to offer. The pool allowed God and man to bathe together, each embraced in the nakedness of the other. Judgment and sin had been banished, or unknown, as both God and man were in their infancies, in their innocence.

Further downstream, another higher falls, Mooney Falls, I would make my way there and beyond in the future. There is a carved-out cave with a window and some steps carved right into the rock that let you out, where a chain ladder takes you down to the base of the falls. Beyond that, you can hike all the way to the Colorado River, just beyond Beaver Falls.

Soon I came to rest creek side and grew sleepy from the sun and exercise. The babbling of the brook lulled me, and I fell off to a deep sleep, and I dreamed I was in this place. Nirvana was to sit in the mist of Havasu Falls on the freshly painted travertine, but an illusion of salvation was on the Hualapai hilltop. For reasons unknown, I could not be content where I sat in nirvana, and I went to find salvation. In this steep, hidden valley, each rock I stepped on crumbled and turned to dust, and the dust washed down and muddied the river. The more I tried to reach salvation, the muddier the river became and the steeper the cliffs grew. I became exhausted from trying and laid down by the bank of the river and was content for the time. When I awoke, I felt beaten, defeated, and decided to attempt the hilltop once again. And the rocks pulverized and washed away, and the river became muddy, and the fresh white paint was stained. I thought salvation could be found another way, and I found myself traveling down the river, away from the hilltop. It was a beautiful and magical land beyond the great falls to an even greater river. There I waited at the confluence of the holy (sacred) creek and the immortal (eternal) river.

Salvation was upstream from here, and that notion, with all of its previous urgency, was just testing my patience and my resolve. Now the rocks did not crumble under my feet, and the earth did not wash down the river, soiling the fresh paint. Every step uphill, sometimes against the rush of the running waters, and after several hours I was back at where I had started, at nirvana, at Havasu Falls. The distance to the immortal river was about the same as to the hilltop, but now I found salvation here, where it had been all along. And the Lord brought me back to peace, and in my contentment, I rested well.

The short respite replenished my well-worn soul. As I had an awakening on the heap in some respects, I had a more personal awakening here in the narrow canyons of Havasupai. I did continue past Mooney Falls and onto the Colorado River, forging back and forth down the creek to the confluence. I felt as if dinosaurs could have been there, hidden from time, deep in that gorge below the reach of civilization.

In a couple of days, I crawled up and out of that sacred land. Once again revitalized and centered. I knew I had masses of people who were looking to me for their own inspiration and guidance. There was also the business of cleaning up the earth that needed tending to, and with my strength and focus, I went to Colorado to take a closer look at some of the superfund sites I had heard about, traveling from one superfund site to another and looking forward to this Rocky Mountain High. Exposing myself to the ultraviolet radiation through the thin tinted glass of the high-elevation atmosphere challenged my resistance to genetic damage and prepped me for my work ahead. Many of the sites were old mining operations, complete with tailings and ponds. Some of them processed radioactive ores and left a warm glow. The soils were contaminated at most of these sites, and the groundwater was spoiled. Remarkably, the wildlife used these open places to regroup and repopulate. Corporate wildlife agents would assure us all that it is perfectly safe and absolutely harmless. They avoided looking at the Gleason scale in the cell samples of the larger mammals to help avoid unwarranted concerns. Ignorance created the only open spaces for our species. Some folks had a lot of it, blue skies.

Lincoln Park was the first site I camped nearby. I liked the name of the place because there is a band called Linkin Park, and they had done some cool stuff. Hiking up between the sixty-eight and the Oak Creek Grade, breathing deep, and boldly sampling the waters I found nearby, finding a relatively flat spot where I could sleep comfortably, I laid my bedroll out. The nights were eerie, and I could feel my skin crawling. Is there still some residual radiation, or was it all in my head? It would be tough to base a case on how I felt, which makes easy work for even the most inept trial lawyers. In the morning, I would make my now-famous yellow cakes and bacon. Just a pinch between my gum and sore, sure to make my ass bleed.

After a week had passed, I had found the place refreshing. If I did not walk north, I would not have seen a single person all week, just what the doctor ordered after the huge crowds two weeks before. From where I was sitting, you could hear cars on the nearby roads and see the lights not so far off. The cooler nights allowed for deeper breathing, and for now, the dismal history was twice removed. The heavens were filled with stars, and the thin crescent moon did not compete but added to the splendor. I wondered if there was any place left on the entire earth that did not need deep cleaning. From the cities to the corn fields, down the highways, to the great outdoors, man left his indelible stain in every boot print. With love and blessings, wrapped his baby in a blanket and abandoned her by his piles of excrement and promised her a better future. You know that future…where we do not kill ourselves solving problems? It is coming soon. I wondered if Moses spent forty years milling around in some man-made desert, and I thanked the Lord for giving me an opportunity to wonder aimlessly for forty of my own years in this industrial desert. I, wrapped in my blanket, am growing old next to these piles of crap. Sometimes my behavior reflects the toxins my forefathers have bequeathed, always attenuating.

Traveling again up Highway 24 to Leadville was easy. I was only on the road for two minutes, and I got a ride all the way up to the California Gulch site. I had no idea how scenic it would be, and some of Colorado's tallest peaks were visible in all their grandeur. The town itself is part of the superfund area, and to me, that was intriguing. In the bigger older cities, you see man tear down and build up in the same location over and over again; somehow it feels different when it had only been built on once, spoiled, and then covered up. I thought of an old industrial site where I had stayed once, and before the EPA investigated the site, they quickly built a mall. Made a huge parking lot and sealed that history in an asphalt tomb. I felt so useless in Leadville; here I was attenuating and doing my best to absorb all the sins of the past, and here I am in a family restaurant. Waitresses and cooks busy running around, the tables occupied by families with children, towns people and travelers, all just living life. Not one of them thought of themselves as attenuators. They would run me out on a rod if they knew my calling. The normalcy was unnerving. We were right in the middle of a superfund site, and life was normalish. I ordered bacon and eggs, as I was starving at this point. The coffee was way above average for a family restaurant. I read all the local brochures they had in the entranceway. Read about all the things to do and the places to go and see. Browsed a few real estate catalogs and was surprised to see how the market was improving and was competitive with many places in the United States. The waitress' name was Molly, and when she was not too busy, we shared a few words. Unlike many of the locals, she was born and raised in Leadville. She did not seem the worse for wear; she was energetic, good complexion, clear-eyed, and very pleasant. She was petite but healthy, looking like she ran or rode a bike for distance. Dirty blond hair and blue eyes, and what I would call sub-alpine tips. When she saw me looking at the camping brochure, she was quick to mention Turquoise Lake and all the camping grounds over there. I told her I would be in town a few days and I would stop back in before leaving town. I could not believe how friendly she was, and actually, the entire staff was pleasant. I always associated metals with anger and fighting…you know poisoned, and lower intelligence and a lack of inhibitors. This did not seem to be the case, and it was encouraging and uplifting, and the thin air added to my Rocky Mountain High.

Another opportunity I had to work on my bucket list was to shop at a grocery store on a superfund site. If you did not know, you would not have been able to tell. All the fruits and vegetables were trucked in, and not a blemish on any of them. The packaged foods looked just like they did in a hundred other stores in which I have shopped. It put me in my prepackaged comfort zone, with products I had been branded by since youth and all the brightly colored choices to keep this child amused. As I left the store, I hung out in front for a little while deciding in which direction I would go next. A guy sat in his car in a handicapped parking space right out the front door with the window down, listening to the radio. Some shock jock was promoting civil war by merely repeating what some other diseased cells had been spewing. He rattled on about Oath Keepers and Proud Boys, sedition, and civil war, and suddenly I felt as if this place could be called Leadville. Violence and ignorance did not rise to the top but sank to the bottom along with the metals. I tried to focus my brain on Molly, but that guy just would not shut up. With such a diseased state, it was not going to take much to incite the patients. It was obvious to even the simple-minded that the political changes were not voicing the will of the people but speaking for the unimpeded greed of the corporate state.

Walking south back out of town proper, I grew angry, Leadville angry. I did not know if it was the lead or being weary from traveling. The environmental issues were more than one man could manage, but how did I allow politics and people to get under my skin? I prided myself on being nondenominational and apolitical, but now I found myself too weak to resist being affected by the banter of propaganda. I found a nice, secluded, toxic flat to roll out my bag and ponder civil war. The California gulch belched promises of a bygone era, a compliment in some cultures. Not paying much attention to Washington, I had no idea the toilet handle had already been depressed. Talk of civil war was on everyone's lips. Political leaders were role models, not in the sense of tradition and honor, but for their primary roles as diseased individuals representing a diseased nation. Simple-mindedness was only a political strategy for the simple-minded. "Strategy" was beyond the intelligence of those cutouts now groomed to command. Like several two-year-old toddlers coveting a shiny object, the nation devolved into envying the man-child with the shiny object.

Laying where I could see a fourteen-thousand-foot peak outlined against a star-filled sky, I thought about the neurology of our nation. I thought about the neural networks and the general health of its brain, spinal cord, and peripheral nerves, and I realized how serious our condition is. The brain is full of plaque and in rapid deterioration; Alzheimer's, Parkinson's, and seizures are rampant. One part of the brain is isolated from other parts and retrieving information becoming impossible. Files lost or dumped, burned libraries of forgotten knowledge, histories being made and asphalted over, the brain is dysfunctional, with the patient in hospice autoimmune diseases set the stage for the proto-onco genes. Exasperated cells were attacking neighboring cells and cleaning house. The myelin sheathing, the insulation on the nerves being attacked and removed, leading to neuropathy, seizures, and eventually organ failure and death. As the diseased state progresses, the patient has difficulties performing even simple tasks. He becomes angry, self-centered, confused, and violent. The nation now, confused, and angry, lashes out at any target without hope of any healing or resolve. Swinging just to swing, hating everything, until he becomes too weak and sick to lash out anymore, not remembering what it was all about in the first place. This gives the corporations an advantage as they do not ask permission or confess sins, especially related to all things that produce profits. Their lifespan will outlive a man's, and what they do not get done today will happen tomorrow. The government needs a high-ketone diet rich in fat to ward off seizures. The fat of the land is now cash, and the seizing officials give the nod to the reapers of the sacred places. As I have been surveying the Garden of Eden, one thing is certain: death is at our doorstep. Neurological dysfunction is the common thread in the American people. Etiologies and pathologies may differ, but for the nervous system in its rapid demise, the results all end with the same morbid outcome. Should a healthy, isolated politician have meaningful words of wisdom and brilliant plans of action, who is healthy enough to hear those words and bear the fruit of those well-conceived plans? Look at the maps of the superfund sites and overlay the chemical plants, overlay the defense plants, and the nuclear facilities. Now add the sprayed forests and farmlands, subtract all the pavement and concrete, sprinkle with 'chem trails, and wrap tightly with a 5G shroud. This is our legacy; this we do to ourselves, to our land, our country, our God. Uncomfortable, I lay wide-eyed into the predawn.

Leadville was a great piece of American pie. People, as normal as the times would allow, survived without struggling. With beliefs that coddled them and their children. Hopes of a promised land at the other end of the bright and eternal rainbow. If you could not handle the truth, there was always a mountain right out the door where one could sit and wait for the freeze. *The things that made America great should not be repeated,* I said to myself as I looked at the train tracks beneath the sifted mountains. I tried to remember Leadville wherever I roamed. The contentment, the ignorance, is bliss; the "Lord saves" of it all. These were the righteous thoughts that comforted them through the days and instilled that fortitude in their children. I needed to learn these techniques and put them into practice.

Having heard so much about Rocky Flats, I had to make a stop by there while I was still in this part of Colorado. Sites like this are of particular interest because they are full of shit. Absolutely safe and perfectly harmless for forty years of downwind victims. Lying war mongers and politicians lived lavish lifestyles on the taxpayers' dime, standing upright on the polyps of the little people. There have been books and movies on the subject, and whether you are an environmentalist, a conspiracy theorist, or an attenuator, these are the stories of evil in the modern landscapes of the American dream that one needs to know. There have been some cleanup attempts, and now a good piece of it is the Rocky Flats National Wildlife Refuge. The plutonium-239 has a half-life of 24,000 years, which is only a concern for the weak-minded. There is no reliable source to determine the health risks in and around Rocky Flats. Our mandated reporters pleading the fifth under threat of repercussions. Carefully designed studies, data acquisition, and controls lead to predetermined outcomes and are used for modeling false narratives.

I could not get into the area where the operational units were because of security issues, but I did attenuate as much of the plutonium as I could in my three days at the wildlife refuge. Once again, it was eerie, and whether it was because I read the books and heard the bullshit or the smell of doom bypassed my cerebral cortex and went directly to my brain stem. "Lord, hear my prayer; may my contaminated body not be the vector that infects my soul. Amen."

As I left Rocky Flats, I was walking along the roadside when a Volkswagen van pulled over and I heard "hop in." It was a man of about fifty-five years old with wild, fro-like hair and metal-framed glasses. He seemed really serious, but as I got in, he broke out in a smile. "I'm Paul," he said.

"I am the attenuator," I responded.

"I knew that. I have seen you before. Actually, I saw you this morning. You used to go by Leper.com, and I used to laugh my ass off seeing some of that. Ever since you went to Oklahoma, you have been on Puritan.com. I appreciate all the work you have been doing. I figured you would be living in Malibu about now, enjoying your newfound fame and chilling like Snoop on the beach."

"I did not know I was still alive. Nobody told me. I have just been going from superfund site to superfund site, attenuating. This place here is devastating. The radiation needs to be remediated, but once again it is the money and the lies need attenuating even more. When you attenuate lies, the truth surfaces; the truth cannot be attenuated but only perpetuated in eternal time and space," I said with conviction.

"So true! I lived here all my life, protested here, and got arrested here. Hey, I was at your sermon on the heap. I traveled down there with a couple friends! I thought it would be like three days at a comedy club…but seriously, I was inspired by your sincerity and motivation. It was so refreshing to hear you speak, especially to all those younger people. I have a renewed belief in people, and there is hope once again within this old pessimist. I have tried for fifty years to have a positive outlook, and in any moment of weakness, I will rant about this ugly life. I always retreat to some altruistic posturing of my younger, undeveloped brain and fight the ugly demons with the energy and strength of my youth," he said as he turned some music on…the first song to play was Donovan's Universal Soldier.

I had not heard that in years, but I sang along with every word. It was remarkable how powerful the words of fifty years ago still were, and Paul asked me, "What'll you do now, my blue-eyed son?"

And those words were a trigger and destroyed the dam that held back a flood of emotion and swept me from the misty mountains to the dozen dead oceans. I could barely speak, but I mumbled, "I dunno."

"Well, I am going out toward Crested Butte for a few days. You are welcome to ride out that way with me if you want. I have got a friend over there. He has got a little cabin; been there for years. Now all these million-dollar homes are sprouting up all over; there is even a Club Med up there. I love that part of the country; in any direction, there are mountains and open space. It is so quiet compared to Denver. I will climb up to twelve or fourteen thousand feet and recharge for a day or two. If I had more time, I would stay longer and do a fasting cleanse. No food, only water, no outside input, no spoken word, no printed word, no radio, no phone, and I direct all my thoughts on accepting and being what is. Being an activist for so long, the hardest part has been trying not to elicit change. Working to diminish the ego's constant need for attention is challenging. Some days are better than others, and some change needs to be invoked."

"That sounds great. I was heading west, so that is perfect. A few days in some cleaner environs is just what the doctor ordered," I said while my mind was still on A Hard Rain.

The music switched up to music and less lyric. I could tell he was a guitar player from his selections, and I was enjoying all the great fret men and all the classic riffs. Some of that Cream, like the ending of White Room, had me gritting my teeth and tightening my muscles. I did not know if three days on the mountains could get that out of my head, but it was therapeutic to be moving on from Dylan and the Hard Rain for the moment.

Paul's friend John lived out by Gothic. I stayed the first night but was anxious to get above the timberline and into the alpine air. I headed out toward the Maroon Bells, as I was told it should be quiet and desolate. The mountains around this part of Colorado were stunning and rejuvenating. The air crisp and clean, the water clear and cold, and the shear ruggedness kept most of man's garbage at bay. As I ascended from Crater Lake, I felt as though I was in the palm of God's hand. I was there with him, and I felt as though I had his undivided attention. He was paying strict attention to the child who had run off and was getting himself into precarious situations, and yet giving him enough room to grow. I could feel his presence on the mountaintops and in the waters below; he was there in the animals and in the plants. He spoke to you in the quaking aspens and among the glacier lilies, broadcasting a delicate contrast to the reds and purples of the dramatic mountains. I had no intention of reaching the summit of Pyramid Peak, and I found a comfortable place to sit in the crumbling mountain debris, a flat coffee table-sized rock sitting level with the valley floor. From this throne, I could feel the earth turning; I could feel this earth ship rushing through space. I could close my eyes and imagine I was at the helm and in command of this vessel, steering it and accelerating through time and space, only to be humbled again upon opening my eyes, feeling as insignificant as of any of God's "lesser" works. My small self-thanked the Lord for listening to me as I asked "why?" a thousand times and answering me with deep, profound silence.

The Standard Mine was another superfund site in Gunnison National Forest, and I thought I would slowly make my way there. Before I did, I wanted to charge myself with one of the oldest and largest living things on the planet. I had heard there was a grove of aspen that was a single organism, where each tree was a sprout from a common root mass and covered over one hundred acres. Almost four and a half million square feet of knowledge and power, of course I was concerned I would contaminate it from being in the trenches, and I also thought it too was an attenuator and would help relieve me of some of my burden. I thought about volunteering at schools, but I did not want to be responsible for making kids sick from being in contact with my poisoned self, so I bowed out gracefully. Here I felt different, as if the Pope came to town, you would have to see him even if you were sick; it was just something you would have to do. It was not like he was a rock star; he was a messenger from God! Heading west from Crested Butte toward Ohio Pass, you could see the grove. You must really give it thought from afar before you enter into its embrace. The age, for one, and then you consider all the events in the last few thousand years, the triumphs and tragedies, plagues and wars, kings, and kingdoms. The genetics that had phylogenetic memories from thousands of years ago, that directed its growth and behaviors for the next few thousand years, which gave it size in terms of more than square feet and weight. Gave it the right to speak from seniority and superior knowledge. Its stoic posture, its mantra of whispering on the wind of dancing foliage and like Jonah, the aspen swallowed me up and in three days spit me out onshore, alive. With renewed faith, I continued my mission.

The Standard Mine site was disappointing in several different ways to me. For one, the site was not massive, at least above ground. I thought most or all American cities had more environmental damage. Here I was, still in the woods, with a small, visible scar on a massive landscape. I did not get into the places and explore tunnels and shafts, and I did not take soil samples to a lab. There were some rusted machines and run-down buildings, but it was still in the woods and there were not many people, so I kind of liked it, but it left me not being on task, and that was the biggest of the disappointments. I did not spend much time there; perhaps I could have looked closer; perhaps there was a lot more I could have done there. I remembered being in a huge rail yard and just shrugging my shoulders, wondering why all the folks who get railroad pension monies do not have to clean up their mess. Passing down the benefits and not the responsibilities, shrug. The day was beautiful, so I hiked west and tried to let go of this one. I tried not to think about what I could help do to remediate, but to focus on the next site and be ready for action when we get there. I stayed out in the woods for a couple of days and eventually made my way to Montrose. The conservative air made me feel like a target. I wondered if any of their portfolios had been damaged by the sermon on the heap. Being a town on the loneliest highway in America, I knew I had more in common with these folks than differences. I did not stay long. I had a good, hot meal with lots of bacon and emulsifiers and got back on the road. Though it was only a little more than one hundred miles, it took me most of a day to get to Uravan, Colorado. This site was more than eight hundred and sixty acres which was a Union Carbide uranium and vanadium mine. A radium recovery plant was started there in 1912. The site was fenced, and warnings of radioactivity were posted along the perimeter. I entered without caution and collected interesting rock specimens. I kicked up some dust and took deep breaths. It had so much more to offer than the Standard Mine site, and I made up my mind to spend at least three days here. I took notes and mapped out a crude map of things that were of interest to me. I asked the Lord for his continuing support and asked to quantify the faith I would need to survive my stay. I am still waiting for a response; sometimes he gets busy. The landscape breathed heavily and pulsated under a blazing sun, in the boot prints of an industrious man, one cannot help but think about war when shriveling in a radioactive waste land. I thought about Americans voting. Did they ever get to vote to go to war? Less than half the people vote, and there are more people than that who are drinkers. One in approximately two people vote, one in four of all Americans is on mental health medications. Almost twelve percent are on drugs; almost six million cannot vote because they were felonized; and more than two percent have autism. It makes one wonder how many voters are actually sane and sober. How many voters' intelligence quota is below average, below eighty, or below seventy-five? These are the people manipulated into putting untrustworthy people in office, the medicated, drunk, idiots. Those patriotic tools that would beat you with a flag if you didn't throw in with them, I tend not to throw in with drugged people, drinkers, war mongers, and idiots; maybe one day I'll come to appreciate the true meaning of a democracy… and start drinking. This irradiated piece of paradise whispered this to me, and I would have kept the secret if I had not become so sick and so near death. I festered, became weak, and moved on.

The Lord is my shepherd, and I, a Dugway sheep en route to a promised land. From Skull Valley, we ascend, always attenuating. The residual radiation from Rocky Flats and the Uravan mining site left me absolutely miserable and sick. The mountains in eastern Utah afforded me the time and space needed to gather my thoughts and my health. My eyes burned throughout the day and night; my gums were bleeding; and some teeth loosened. I was half covered in festering sores and too confused to function. I held up eating pine nuts, forbs, and Mormon crickets. Some of the

Mormon crickets I roasted on a fire; some of them I preserved by drying in the sun or soaking them in vinegar. The swarms were of biblical proportion, manna from heaven, and though I had no appetite, I forced myself to eat, hoping to regain a viable brain if nothing else.

As I convulsed on a desolate and barren talus slope, a stream of consciousness revealed my hopes and fears. It was hard to say if it were the isolation, the near death (again), or a diet rich in protein and minerals, but all I could think about was procreating and leaving descendants. I had found other biologic purposes in being an attenuator, but here alone on this barren eminence, progenerating became of the gravest import. Neglecting and ignoring, stifling what many profess as the sole purpose of life, vanished from my horizons as my own finish line sprinted toward my rapid decline. It was not too late to do something about my future and my legacy. I meditated and spent time trying to have a singular focus on my scattered thoughts. It made sense to me to go to a sperm bank and make huge deposits with hopes and prayers of progeny. A bevy of the faithful, blessed attenuators in the chilly night, on the barren slope, it had been decided. As if I were a teenager in love, I was filled with joy and happiness and a renewed sense of purpose, one that was filled with promises of life on earth. For a moment, I was able to shed the morbid, terminal earthly future I, the Attenuator, had embraced. Always the promise of an afterlife, rarely content in the moment. Never not working, inhale, exhale…attenuating.

The next morning, I got back on the road, setting my sights on Salt Lake City. To me, there was not a better place to put seed up. The genealogical data base the Mormon

Church researched and libraries are state-of-the-art. I started getting a little manic, thinking all the good things that await. They might even have use for my seed, as it has become resistant to toxins. Maybe I am the cure for cancer. Maybe they will want to spread my seed far and wide; this is not just any seed…this is The Seed from the Attenuator. My head grew to house an ever-expanding ego. It is not just my future or my progeny; this is the future of mankind. When I got closer to the city, I got on a bus, and it took me right to where I wanted to be. I felt as distant to the person sitting next to me as I did to someone on the east coast. I did not want to be that distant, but I thought those were the rules of social aggregates. Of course, there had to be that one guy… who recognized me from Puritan.com, here in the land of the Mormons, and he immediately took a picture of me and was on the website sharing it with the people in front of the bus. He was clean-shaven and dressed in his Sunday best. I remembered this was not Leper.com anymore, so they were not here to ridicule and make fun of me but to be uplifting and inspirational. He asked me for an autograph, and I gave him and five or six others my signature, The Attenuating Puritan. I was embarrassed to be going to a sperm bank, but I did not tell anyone about my new mission.

The building was modern, with stone and glass. It was a couple stories tall and right in the heart of the city. To my relief, it did not advertise with "sperm bank" in neon lights, and there was no signage to know this was the place. The first thing I saw when I walked in was the receptionist. Immediately, I had a lump in my throat. She was young, attractive, pardon me for saying "hot" and a smiling brunette. She was wearing a button-up starched white blouse and a gray skirt that was plain and cut to just below the knees. She was full-chested, bright-eyed, with the brightest red lips. I had walked in like a rooster but lost my edge on seeing her. Here she was at work, comfortable at a sperm bank, a place I could never imagine myself being, and she was eager to help. I thought I must have died and gone to heaven. I stared at her lips as she said some words. She spoke clearly and articulately, but I could not hear the words as she continued her subliminal seduction. There were stacks of papers to fill out, and I sat at a table and worked on them, looking over at her every thirty seconds or so. After most of an hour had passed, I returned the stack to her. Soon an older gentleman came from behind a closed door. He may have been a doctor. "I am Robert Smith; I go by 'Bob,'" he said. Just then, a shorter, middle-aged woman came out from behind the same door.

"I am Gabriella Day," she said and pleasantly extending a hand to shake.

"We will be doing all the lab work. I see this is your first time; have you banked anywhere else?" he asked.

"No, this is my first time," I answered.

"Do you have any questions now?" he asked.

I was too nervous to speak and kept glancing over at the beauty at the desk, who was intentionally smiling provocatively, playfully enjoying my tension.

"No, I don't think so," I awkwardly responded.

They had all seen my type before, and Gabriella told me to get comfortable. *They are like machines*, I thought to myself… they do this all day long, every day. I felt scarred from my childhood Catholicism, stunted, and repressed.

Even that gorgeous receptionist sits there all day and takes it…I think I am going to like this… I will be a regular.

Gabriella escorted me to a private room, handed me a small container, and told me to get it all in there. Here are a couple of magazines, and there is a movie on there now. If you need more to help you, let us know. I wanted to ask now, "What if I grow hair on my palms," "what if I go blind," "what if my thing falls off?" but I filled out my chest and, like a red-blooded stud, said, "I'll be fine." While the movie played, all my thoughts were about that receptionist, and being all business without pleasure, I was done in an instant (actually, it was about ten good minutes). There was a cubbyhole where the cup was to go that had a back door, sort of like a Nathan's coin-operated eating establishment. I put my cup up, and I was done. It was easier to look at the receptionist on the way out. She told me they would freeze it and then screen it for viability in a couple of days. There were a lot of cancer patients banking, and I just assumed I was the perfect candidate for their service.

Having three or four days, I thought I would get outside the city and find a clandestine place to hold up. It was surprising to see how much open space was within hours of the city. It was easy to find a place to disappear for a few days. I do not know how clean it was, but there was plenty of water around. I had some food now, but still did not have an appetite. I had a trash bag like I always do, but the place I hid had relatively little trash. There was some along the highway, but after leaving the thoroughfare, the landscape was fairly clean. For most of the three days, I slept and slept some more. All I could think about was going back and seeing that receptionist and doing more banking. Again, my sores were healing quickly, and my liver had not been troubling me at all. My hair was still falling out, and my stigmata had new coats of fresh paint, but I did not feel like I had on that barren slope where death was around the next corner. I was more alive; I was full of hopes and dreams.

Friday came, and it was time for me to go back to the fertility clinic. I was excited; it seemed like the biggest day of my life. Packing up my few things and laying the place to rest, I made my way back to the road. Beethoven ran through my head in an inspiring an uplifting way. I hummed off-key and off-tempo, but it worked for me. Sticking my thumb out again, I was hoping I would get a ride before I saw a cop. All things were great, as I got a ride in the first ten minutes. It was not a ride…it was a portal to another dimension. A guy named Flash was driving, and next to him sat Paisley. Flash was about six feet, one or two, and a hundred and sixty pounds. He had shoulder-length, light brown hair wrapped up in a bandana. His eyes were dilated and wide. He laughed indiscriminately, and energy could be seen sparking from his thin frame. Paisley's eyes were dilated, but she did not speak a word. Her eyes darted around, and she oozed paranoia. When everyone else laughed, you could hear her breathing deep and gripping the dashboard. In the back behind the driver was Space, and now in the middle, Sunshine, I sat behind Paisley. Space and Sunshine were also wide-eyed and in hysterics. I did not know what was so funny, and for a few minutes I thought it must have been me. Space finally told me what I had suspected…they were all frying. They had left New Jersey three days ago and had been dosing on supposedly pure lysergic acid diethylamide, Space had told me in between repeating the word Hoboken, over and over again in a voice mimicking a car horn. Flash and Sunshine barked back with "Hoboken," and they laughed uncontrollably. It was funny, but not that funny, and I was fearing for my life as Flash was way too high to drive. It was no wonder Paisley was digging her fingers into the dash and scared speechless. She knew she was in the suicide seat.

We were inside the city limits, and I was close to my destination. I did not get a lot of conversation out of any of them, but the little bit I did get let me know they were cool peace and love promoters, wanting to make love, not war. We were burning a joint and blasting Pink Floyd when suddenly there were flashing lights behind us. There was no looking normal, not even close. Flash slowed down, and Paisley managed an "oh shit." Space and Sunshine were like routine five, and he ripped out three glass jars of pure acid and said, "Here," and handed me one. He also gave me a small bag with a few random pills. I do not know if I was trying not to get busted or just adept at attenuating, but I downed mine in one swift gulp, and then the bag of pills. Both Space and Sunshine downed an entire jar, and that is some record dosages. The cops rolled in thick, and backup had already arrived. What was unusual were the Federal Bureau of Investigation guys that were on the scene. We all got out of the car and stood on the side of the road as they rifled through the vehicle. Sunshine and Space got rid of their empties, but mine was on the floor in the back. I am sure it had some residues that could be tested. They found a little weed but did not seem to be content with that. They pulled the seats out and took the door panels off; you could tell they were really pissed. One of the Feds took me to the side and said, "We know you are not with them. We have been following them since New Jersey; we listen to all their phone calls; we know what they are carrying; we also know who you are, and if I were you, I would just start walking." I wanted to get out of there, but I also did not want them to think I ratted them out.

I looked at Space and let him read my lips: "They've been following you." and I walked away. It was the last I ever saw of any of them. I am sure they were going to be all right; cops did not get much, and they were smart enough to lawyer up when needed. We were all bozos on that bus.

So, my day began, and I made it down to the clinic. I was just starting to get off, so I was trying to get the important stuff done before I could not. The receptionist had a visible aura around her and was pulsating at the desk. She looked at me and looked down at her desk, and a minute later Bob and Gabriella came in. I could feel something was not right, and it was not just the acid…this could have been a beautiful trip…

"I am sorry to inform you that you are infertile. There are few non-motile sperm and ninety percent necrozoospermia. This means most of your sperm cells are dead, and it would be, at this point in time, not a good decision to bank them. We can discuss options to help improve your overall health and virility. We have had many successes in fertility cases, but you must also know, many times we do not get the results we hope and pray for. As his arm moved down at his side, I saw huge trails, and I was too high to process what was being said. I heard him; I knew what he meant, but I did not know what it meant to me or what my next move would be. I told them both I wanted to come back in a couple of weeks to see if I could do anything for my future. He told me, "Yes I could come back; make sure you're not using drugs or smoking." He walked over to the rack on the wall, handed me some brochures, and told me to read them. With that, I was left sinking and sailing simultaneously. As low as one could be and as high as one could be. The second time today someone was speechless, and when I could finally talk, I said the same exact thing, "Oh shit!"

I walked by the receptionist's desk, gave her the saddest dilated puppy eyes, and hung my head, saying, "I'll be back."

As I headed out toward the entrance, for some reason I took the stairs that were off to the right. I descended into a lower floor, which had several doors off the main entryway. Beneath the stairwell was a half-closed-in area, and I ducked in there. I was perspiring, and my heart was racing. Some of the pills that I had eaten must have been blue, as I had a strong erection, the like of which I had not known. All my emotions were amplified to extremes, and I was depressed and angry, and I asked the Lord, "How could you do this to me? I thought we were cool." I started rubbing myself, at first just touching, then stroking. I had my robe pulled up around my waist and was frantically jacking off the entire time I was talking to God. "Son of God IS the son of man; son of man IS the Son of God. Son of God IS the son of man, son of man IS the Son of God. Fruit of the womb, fruit of the womb, fruit of the womb." As I came, I yelled, "Begat, begat, begat!" One orgasm wasn't going to fix my sunken sailors, and I was determined to repair my broken machinery, yanking my still rock-solid crank and repeating the mantra, "Son of God is the son of man, son of man is the Son of God, Son of God is the son of man, son of man is the Son of God. Begat, begat, begat." The emotional frenzy, the acid, the pills, the infertility, I do not know which of these factors was responsible for my robe putting on a show. In uniform randomness, every other pixel lit up and then blackened for a split second, followed by the adjacent pixels lighting and blackening, which created a strobe effect. I heard footsteps in the foyer above me and thought I should retreat into one of the more concealed locations behind one of the doors. I was fortunate enough to have the first doorknob I tried turn and open up into a larger storage area. The room was filled with furniture, filing cabinets, and miscellaneous boxes. I found myself hiding in the back of the room, stroking and strobing, "Son of God, son of man…Begat, begat." And thinking of the receptionist, who knew I came to cum, "Fruit of the womb."

For a full three days and nights, I masturbated non-stop. It was not until the morning of Tuesday that I left the clinic stained in semen and smelling like goats. My eyes were burning, I had rubbed new raw spots, and I do not know if I fixed my broken toy/tool. I just wanted to get as far away from Salt Lake City as I could, and I headed west again. California sounded like the place to go for now. I was not in "mission" mode; I was in escape mode. I could not believe my hopes of progeny were being challenged, and all my bold attenuation had consequences. The Lord really let me down this time, and it was not gentle. I told myself, "Put your robe on like a big boy, and one sandal in front of the next." It was half a day later, I was in Nevada. The next ride I got was with a woman named Violet. She was heading to

Elko, where she lived. She told me she worked as an entertainer, and I assumed she mostly did casino gigs, but what do I know. I asked, "Are you married?"

"I was, but it didn't last too long," she said. My husband wanted kids…and I could not have any." She sighed when she said that.

I do not know what made me speak up. I usually am not so open, but I said, "I can't either."

"I guess there are a lot of us these days, and you see who gets to have children, the ones that do not want or do not take care of them. I thought about adopting, but with my history, they would make it difficult," she said.

"What history?" I asked.

"Well, right now I work at a brothel, and I did not always have the luxury of a safe work environment. When I first started, I was on the street. I did not have any folks to go to. It was really bad," she said.

"Sorry," I said.

"You don't have to be sorry; sometimes I make bad choices; sometimes life just sucks," she said, grinning and licking her lips.

"Yeah, I guess I made some bad choices too, and you are right, sometimes life just sucks. I had been attenuating, you know, cleaning up toxins using my body to filter them out, and the next thing I know, I cannot have kids," I said.

"Wow, I guess we are cut from the same cloth. Both used our bodies to make a better world and got bit in the ass for it," she said humorously.

"I still have hopes; the Lord usually works with me. I will try to behave for a while and see if my health improves," I said.

"Well, I hope it does," she said as her eyes reached out.

She let me out on the west side of Elko so I could keep moving on. I would swear I knew her from somewhere, maybe a past life.

The next ride was like spaceship earth. Here I was again, forgetting all about yesterday and attenuating my ass off. Who knows, who cares, destination unknown. From there, I do not remember much.

In these demanding and impatient times of uncertainty, faith was my Sherpa. Though the microcosm of fellowship was an obex to divinity, to witness the one percenters mingling with the residual ninety-nine, all attenuating the irradiated sands of Nevada, was truly a testament to unity.

My eyes ached as each, and every muscle was strained and taxed. They were hard, gritty, dry, and stinging, and could not rest or settle. I had to rest my fingertips on the lids to keep them closed. Yet somehow images appeared sharper than ever before, purpose and direction no longer needed to be pondered. An electric epiphany like the cosmic awakening that brought the polymerase chain reaction to Kari Mullis.

The ebb and flow of the competing noise in the background, seventy thousand people whispering rhubarb, offset by an invasive electrical buzz like a large, damaged transformer, only to fade away to my own heartbeat and cerebral confusion.

"Hey, are you all right?" I deciphered from that pervasive roar.

"What?" I answered instinctively, but what I really meant was…are you talking to me?

Repeating the question, "Are you all right?" anchored me to the earth by an ear.

Though I felt as if I were floating, I soon realized I was laying on a cot.

"Where am I?" genuinely not knowing.

"You, my friend, are at Burning Man! You are in the trip tent!" said as if I had won some badge of honor.

"WOW! Far, far out! I love you all, man!" triggering the memory that there had been heaping helpings of ecstasy with the acid in the attenuators' rations. It immediately turned to a quick chill, imagining Shulgin working for Bayer/Monsanto. *The devil does excellent work*, I said to myself.

There were several people in the "room" when a tall young man entered. He was three or four days unshaven, wearing lights, beads, bangles, expensive sunglasses, and a dab of sunscreen on his nose.

"I am Doctor Tim," he said as he placed a hand on my shoulder.

"Doing better now?" he said, laughing.

Naturally, I wondered what fool I played, but for a seasoned vet like me, it had become the norm.

"Yes, I am fine, thanks. My mission takes me on many strange and dangerous adventures," I said.

"Tell me about that," he said, sounding like an old therapist of mine.

In a voice like that of an older British Shakespearean actor, I said, "I ask the Lord, oh gracious God, how may I serve you? How may this humble and feeble servant adorn your splendid gardens? My only purpose and my only identity are as your servant. And though I have sinned (whispering "Hail Mary") I am pure; I am a puritan; I am The Attenuating Puritan…and though I am pure in thought, word, and deeds, my behaviors occasionally reflect the toxins my forefathers have bequeathed me."

Reaching for something to drink to wash the desert sands down, "Oh God, must I do the deeeeeeewwwww. Brominated vegetable oil binds to my iodide receptors and attenuates in my thyroid, mimicking schizophrenia, God damn it! Forgive me, Lord, for my sin. Attenuating, I have been bled by the microwaves and have transcriptions of errant code, Amen."

Continuing, "Through self-awareness, God, your image has become clearer. In my mind's eye, we become as one. An ungraven image of Mohammed, the sum product of light in subtractive color theory and in an attempt to get closer to thee through ritual fluoridations, your image becomes shrunken and fades. Good Lord, you have endowed me with a pineal gland the size of a grapefruit; I am uncertain if it is engorged from fluoride attenuation or a gift from you of true spiritual wealth."

Doctor Tim interrupted, "Do you think you can stand, now?"

"Good Lord willing," the Attenuator replied.

He swung his legs off the cot, and his soles touched the floor as he pivoted into a sitting position. The floor was grounding, and he could feel the energy running through his body, down his legs, and arcing through the thin fabric and into the earth. Pushing with both hands, he raised himself, and Doctor Tim steadied him.

"What a rush!" he said as the blood redistributed.

"You had better eat something," Doctor Tim suggested. "You have no doubt depleted all your essential nutrients."

I nodded as I took the first step. From the side where Doctor Tim stood, he could see dried blood on the back of the attenuators robe, and he bent around to see the back in its entirety. There, upside down and looking up, was the face of Jesus, like the Shroud of Turin. The eyes followed and seemed to be looking right at you, no matter where you stood. Upon his seeing, an awkward moment of silence and a feeling of light and warmth as the blessedness embraced him. Kneeling before his theanthropic master, he asks, "How may I serve you?"

"To kneel before me is blasphemous. I, too, am merely a servant. Do God's work. Keep sacred even the smallest of God's creatures; exalt the dogma of the living. For in that ancient wisdom, a kingdom awaits."

From this moment on, these two lives forged an inseparable bond, bound in the strappings of purpose, direction, humanity, and an unflagging devotion to God.

"I wear the robe of repentance, and my sins shall be revealed."

The light got brighter as the tent flap opened. An intimidating golden alien entered. Gold from head to toe. A golden pointed pontiff's crown, a gold painted face, gold long and pointed conical breast covers, golden shorts, with golden leggings, and thigh-high golden boots Bracelets and charms dangled from her ears and arms. Gold on her shoulders and around her waist, hanging from her crown. The tremendous flash of light from the sun as she entered left me with the impression I was among Egyptian royalty.

Short and sweet, she barked, "Doctor we need more!"

He glanced at me, rolled his eyes, and made his way to a little locked cabinet. He scribbled on a little sheet of paper and handed it to her. Searching through the keys on an overloaded key ring, he found the one and unlocked the cabinet. He proceeded to count out a vial full of pills and handed them over to her. "Here you go Aura," he said.

I looked into her eyes, and she quickly looked away. Of course, I was hoping she was attenuating, but I knew she was just partying. I wanted to say something to her…but I let it go.

I could see in Doctor Tim, professional shame, it was doubtful he had ever felt it before. Enabling was not the Lord's work, and he knew that.

As I shook off the poisons, I told the doctor it was nice to meet, and I would make a point of seeing him before I left. Still half out of my mind, I walked aimlessly around the electric carnival. Part of the time I felt as if I were in a Klee and half the time in a Bosch. Each and every face etched itself into a retrievable image on the tip of my cerebrum. As I worked my way from camp to camp, marveling at the sights all the while picking up trash, I saw her again.

She was with a young girl, and now bold and flirty, she said, "Hi! Remember me?"

"Yes, you were in the medical tent," I responded, glad to finally connect with someone in the buzzing crowd.

"I am Aura, and this is my daughter, Newday. Where are you staying? You should camp with us; it will be fun!" she brazenly asked.

"I am the Attenuating Puritan," I meekly responded. "I do not have any camp, tent, or even a sleeping bag. I really appreciate the invite," I told them.

"The doctor told me all about you," she said, smiling and batting her eyelashes. "He was impressed with you. Is it true what he was saying about you?" she said grabbing my arm and snuggling up to me.

"I do not know, but I doubt it," again replying meekly.

"He said you are the one!" she enthusiastically spouted.

I laughed and said, "I am merely a servant. I would be humble and grateful if you could offer me respite as I am weary from the deviations off the narrow path."

The music seemed visible. The stars more plentiful than ever before. The Milky Way a pasty swatch across the black gesso canvas. The smells wafting from the camp kitchens had me salivating and realizing how long it had been since I had any nourishment. I continued picking up trash as they danced and howled all the way back to their encampment.

As the moon was new, I took to prayer, immediately raising up an offering of my blood and skin cells in a burnt offering. Surrendering living parts of myself seemed most appropriate for my small congregation of one. I had become accustomed to this ritual. There was wisdom in many of the ancient practices. From our own Indigenous peoples to the agnihorta, Steiner's theosophical teachings, to the Old Testament Hebrew observances, man's knowledge was practiced in ritual.

"Dear Lord, accept these gifts from your most humbled servant. I plea for the strength to carry your task to fruition and to teach that it may be so in this Garden of Eden into eternity."

"With every breath…attenuating."

"With each and every thirst that is quenched…attenuating."

"With every gift from thy bounty…attenuating."

"Purity through me…Amen."

Aura had observed the prayer and was high enough or horny enough to show some interest.

"Do you pray often?" she asked.

"Yes, increasingly these days. Though I strive to embrace all things living, as of late I have been troubled by corporations, invasive species, and tolerance. Tolerance is a measure of turbidity and erodes the cornerstones of civilization. Remember always, "Too much freedom is a curse!" I spoke.

She was now sitting very close, touching my leg, and smelling like a field of wildflowers.

"I hate corporations! They are fucking everything up! I wish we could go back to the old days and live on the land. We would have everything we need right there, all our food and all our building materials. I have always dreamed of being on a farm," she said wishfully.

"That would be the life. Let's go," I said half-joking.

"Where do you live?" she asked.

"I have just been wondering around doing the Lord's work. Last I remembered, I was walking the railroad tracks from Rocky Flat to Livermore, just praying for the strength to defy testicular cancer as I stepped from tie to tie. Aside from the creosote, the easements were sprayed regularly, and there is much attenuating to do along those tracks," I told her.

Her head was now on my shoulder, and her fingertips were making little circles further and further up my thigh. Her speech was soft and slurred.

"Where were you born?" she asked.

"On the east coast," I said, "outside of New York City. A wonderful place to grow up, truly blessed," I said. I always can tell from that accent, and she said New Yawk, like she was from Jersey.

I was now fully aroused and looking to redirect her.

"I always think of this scenario when I look at tolerance…a sexually liberated, inebriated, foul-mouthed, tatted, and pierced biker chick wearing remnants of the sacred cow lights up a smoke, smelling like alcohol, meth, and fossil fuels, then tells me how fucked up I am for not supporting the troops…and I think to myself, not even soldiering distances you from discarded lives as thoroughly as does the python of pop culture. Only sedition can kill the serpent," I said without being able to redirect.

Her hand had made it to my penis, and she giggled. "I have a couple of tattoos!"

She was eager to show them and started unbuttoning her top and pulling down the bottoms.

"This is the first one I got," she said enthusiastically. It was a couple of cherries on the stem, south and sinister to her navel.

I was relieved my robe did not blacken from desire, though I felt it should. No harm, no foul. There were roses, lilies, butterflies, hummingbirds, Celtic knots, and a couple of names and dates. I had the complete guided tour of her canvas with an exclusive artist narrative.

"Tattoos are part of the dance of the salted slug, amplifying a universal contempt and an individual discontent. Vanity is part of one of the seven deadly sins, a part of pride. In man's macrocosm of ego, vanity is the apex. The ego feeds the need for self-expression and self-gratification, demonstrating a lack of faith and victimization by a militarized and failing capitalist society. With a childlike mentality, we took the crayons to everything, for nothing is sacred. Our taxed nervous systems do not allow content. Some of the world's most beautiful models flaunt the marks of the beast."

Continuing the rant, "When skin is pierced, immunoglobulin IgE races into action. It has a half-life of about forty-eight hours, partly because it is such a toxic substance. Anaphylactic shock is a reaction to this immunoglobulin's environment. The constant punctures abuse this natural and necessary defense system and leave those with overtaxed immune systems vulnerable to the next opportunistic disease. Many of the inks can also produce allergic reactions. Once again, letting the ill-informed youth, without the aid of executive functioning, bring it to pop culture and another void, where the cries of contempt diffuse and dissolve."

As I was rambling on Newday interrupted with, "Hey Mom, can I use your lipstick?"

She had the perfect bean body. Standing firmly on the ground, buttocks in the east, beautiful supple breasts in the west, her head held high with dignity and confidence. Seven senses of seduction catabolized my inhibitions. Aura popped a couple more pills and offered me a few, which I dutifully attenuated. I remembered the blue ones from Salt Lake City.

My procreator was still in her hand when she said, "Go ahead, Honey."

The nymph, the herquitic, and the Puritan retired to the tent, acknowledging the Lord for these earthly pleasures.

Aura teasingly said, "Do you want my daughter?"

My robe blackened immediately as I said, "No!"

"I want you to cum in my mouth," Newday sans inhibitors spoke. And Aura was enthralled with the seduction. The carnal pleasures continued into the eep hours when we succumbed to exhaustion and lay spent. I felt blessed, squeezing them both, drifting in and out, thanking God.

The sun was baking the tent, and Newday was shaking me and screaming frantically. Her mom unresponsive, lay lifeless next to me. Even with great faith, hopelessness exuded, and darkness wrapped us fully in a shroud. She was rushed to the medical tent, and it was my friend, Doctor Tim, who pronounced her deceased.

A week had passed, and the tents were all rolled up. The attenuators went on with their lives when the news bore what we already knew: fentanyl, cocaine, oxys, and alcohol. Like so many, aspirated in her own vomit. With some disgust and empathy, we asked the Lord to let her rest in peace. I felt guilty for not eating more of her pills and drinking more of her alcohol, but only in a selfish moment; deep down, I knew it was her time and there was a master plan.

Newday and I headed out to California, trying hard not to look back but keeping her memory present. The non-native, rare, and endangered sub-species trimmagrintus califomicus were heading over to the coast, and we rode with the crew to some northern California ghost town. On the ride, I detailed the revelation in the trip tent. God had spoken to me, directing me in my life work. Take a wife, and she would be Eve, and through us both, purity. Through us, Eden would be pure. We left the trimmers at a health food store, and from there we walked to the center of town. We sat in a park for an hour and got a plan together. A couple of skaters flew by, and I waved them down. "Hey, do you have a phone I can borrow for a sec?" I asked.

"Sure," the one kid answered.

"Thanks man," I said.

I looked up Puritan.com…and it redirected me to my old name, Leper.com. It seems my stint in Salt Lake City was enough to demote the Puritans. There were blurred-out videos of me in the basement of the clinic, which was very unbecoming. Once again, they were offering cash incentives for the stupidest shit I was doing. I was so glad I shed my robe when I was with Aura. I showed the kids that site, and they thought it was pretty f…ing funny. Then I got back to business and looked on Craigslist for a ride down to the Bay Area. That only took a couple minutes, and I had us a ride lined up. The ride was supposed to go all the way to Sunnyvale, but about an hour after we were on the road, he got a call that was important enough to make him turn around and head back north. We did not mind; we were travelers, and change was the constant. With every step and each passing second, the movements of the earth and the seeming motionless heavens all promoted change and kindled our adventurous spirits.

We sat on the side of the road just south of Bumfuct and did not even bother to stick out our thumbs. After a while, we tried hitchhiking and started walking with our thumbs out. Knowing there were towns just up ahead, we picked up our pace. It had been a couple of hours, and we were hungry, thirsty, and still had not landed a ride. Some days are better than others; I could not remember waiting so long to get a ride, especially in an area known for hippies and liberalism. There is always a reason…and as we continued, Newday spotted a large contractor bag filled with weed. It was predominantly shake but had some good nuggets and lots of littles. Our resources were low, and for this gift, we gave thanks to the Lord. Like the rock of triumph, it outweighed the rock of shame. And we carried it along the highway and into the next town, giving more of ourselves to the bag than what was reciprocated. As we entered into the village, there were the usual gas stations and mini marts competing for business at the entry ways of the town, and even in my hunger, I made a strong-willed effort to avoid these places. I spoke with a local and asked him where there was some "good" food. He pointed up the street, saying there was a little hippie market up the road about a half mile. He said it was a little organic food store and cultural center for the counterculture. Heading in that direction, we knew we were getting close when we began to hear a hang drum, hanging hypnotic and pseudo-enchanting melodies on the oppressively hot, thin air. I wanted to hear Bach played on a hang drum; I always wondered if his music would cause piloerection if played on kazoos or slide whistles. The smell of sage and patchouli wafted my way, and I could see some dreadlocks up ahead. There was a comfort zone surrounding the place, as there always is. Motherly types mixed in with intellectuals, conspiracy theorists, and electric deadhead vagabonds would make the pilgrimage to Mecca at the Guru's Grainery. I was one of these folks, and it was stimulating to be back among those folks in those elements. We read every post on the bulletin board. Lost pets, handymen looking for work, rooms for rent, lots and lots of land for sale, remnants from Mom and Pop dino-grows, orgasmic meditation, a post-pandemic, new-age slice of the sixties.

We went in and grabbed a few things: kefir, a fist full of granola bars, and a bulk sack of gorp. The last few times I had purchased nuts, there was a cancer warning on the label, and though I was an attenuator, something about the printed word made them much more difficult to digest. Without the warning, they were savory; with the warning…not so much. There was a bench outside in the shade, so we sat there drinking kefir and munching on the "real" savory gorp. Soon a hacky sack landed on the bench right next to Newday, and a young man ran up, apologizing. "No problem," Newday and I said in unison.

"You want to burn one?" he asked. We could tell he was cool, and I wondered if he had seen our small sack of littles.

"Sure," I said, appreciating the invite.

"Let's not light up right in front of the store, we can sit over there by that creek," he said.

I had not noticed there was a creek less than a stone's throw to the south. It had a little bridge and passed right under the main street.

"Yeah, they would probably appreciate that," I said as we walked over and sat beneath the bridge on the side of the little creek. We were close enough to the store that we could still hear the hang drum, which became ever more enchanting against the background of gurgling waters.

"I'm Dino," he said. "I think this is sherbanger, but it could be the slurz; I rolled a couple of each this morning." He dry-hit it and said, "This is slurz," and passed it over to me.

I dry-hit it and lit it. The first hit was transcending; it was more than a doob it was an experience. I coughed and hacked, and he laughed. "Sales cough?" he said.

"Wow!" I choked out "That is perfectly dank." I said with a short breath, trying not to cough. "This is Newday; I am Puritan; I am an attenuator. I have been trying to clean up toxic sites one small piece at a time. I had no idea when I started how much we have poisoned ourselves, our bodies, and our earth. Shitting in your own backyard is a sign of both affluence and arrogance. I could tell you stories…" I was saying.

"See this creek, looks harmless enough; this is Bechtel Creek. I had a friend who lived up here, died two years ago from brain cancer. This creek is where a plating company disposed of its toxic waste from the nineteen forties right into the nineteen nineties. There has been lots of cancer; in fact, it is a cancer "hot spot." For our relatively small population, we have a relatively high percentage. There was a fund to build that hospital up the road, but one stipulation was that they could not investigate the causes of the cancer. Everybody knows, nobody says."

"On main street, next to a health food store…I got to drink some of this. I will just pull a little of the toxins out and run them through my divine filters. The Lord will have my back," I said with conviction.

"I wouldn't! Don't, don't, don't do it," Dino said panicking.

But it was too late, and I was on all fours, bent down with my face in the creek, and drinking big gulps with big faith.

Newday said, "He always does that."

"Doesn't taste bad. I cannot even taste the metals, but I do feel like hearing some Megadeth," I said, blistering tongue in blistering cheek.

"You're fucking nuts!" he said, not knowing whether to laugh or cry. As I had knelt before the creek, he saw the inverted image of Christ on my robe. He saw it was painted in blood, and the eyes would follow. From that epiphany, salvation, and another attenuator was christened.

"If we all just do a little to clean up and put an end to making these invisible and unspeakable messes, there may yet be a future for man and this earth. That is not my call, but I can hope; I can believe in tomorrow," I told him. "This is just one business; we spray the forests; there are 'chem trails raining down; spray the world with round-up and poison our foods by making them resistant to those poisons. I just came back from some nuclear waste lands that are now deemed "safe" and have become a wildlife refuge. Is there any end to the fuckery from those politically correct predators? The economy is more important than life itself. It is an earthly honor, superficial and temporary, that one could be so far removed from all that is sacred."

We continued smoking and drinking, and Dino joined me for a sip of that cool, clear creek. We discussed the state of affairs. He, too, felt a sense of doom. I think anyone who has lived in the nuclear age has that same gnawing fear. I had heard neurotic was removed from the medical terminologies because it was no longer a symptom but part of the norm. Living in fear of nukes, taking for granted the risks of driving, living under transmission lines, being glued to a cell phone, the neurosis is just weakness and does not belong in the military industrial complex. You kind of owe it to your neighbor to die from consumer goods. Dino heard the message, and I believed he would tell one other person, which would tell one other attenuator.

We parted ways, and Newday and I walked to the south end of town, and I put my thumb out. We got a ride shortly thereafter with an older woman who was going to Santa Rosa. I thought she was living dangerously, picking up hitchhikers, but she was optimistic and strong in her faith. She was also hoping for some excitement in her life, and I do not think we were able to provide that for her. She dropped us off at a park-and-ride place and told us we could catch a bus down into the city from there. It was maybe fifteen minutes before a bus arrived, and we continued south. When we got to the north bay, we could see large plumes of smoke towering toward the stratosphere. Dark clouds charging upwards, like pillars supporting the skies on the southern shore of the bay. There were at least a dozen columns, some of which were the sum of several fires. The bridge was closed going over to Richmond, and it made me wonder what it would be like in that area, since that was our destination. The bus was going to San Francisco, and we continued into the city. We would hopefully circumvent any problems by taking the Bay Bridge over to Oakland.

I had always had a fondness for San Francisco, usually spending my time on the west side, hanging by the Pacific along the great highway. I was not going to let a stay in the Mission District impose itself on my already established views of the city. I had been around enough to know one had to be vigilant. I also knew the Lord had my back and my mission was his, and it gave me a sense of fearlessness. I knew people to some degree, and I was sure disheartened by what I saw there. The same homeless type camps as Flint, tent cities like Oklahoma City or Burning Man, but they were set up on the sidewalks, on the pavement, in front of stores and businesses. Void of the smallest inkling of health and safety. A stench of addiction glued them to their source and fettered them just beyond the reach of knowing the great outdoors. Fouling their air with smoke, their water with plastic, and their hopes with drugs. Once again, as an attenuator, I was overwhelmed. Needles scattered abundantly outside tents on the sidewalks. Piles of stolen merchandise rapidly exchanged for favors. Rainbow fentanyl like sidewalk chalk, no longer out of sight, out of mind, but overtly advertising to the next generation. Somewhere near here is where shame had been buried.

Like Santa Claus, I gave away a fistful of weed at every occupied space. Newday carried a bag for picking up trash, and we picked up needles, feces, and shit. When her bag outweighed our weed stash, we switched bags, and by the end of the day, we were out of care packages. We had picked up six full bags of trash and disposed of them.

Early evening, we went to get some food; we were both starving as we had not eaten all day. We found a place that, according to the word on the street, had decent food and plenty of it. It was a Guatemalan place, remarkably simple and plain. No carpets, no drapes, no table clothes, plastic chairs on tiled floors, and cafeteria tables…the food was out of this world, and we could not have found a better place to eat. The people were genuine, and we were able to have some enjoyable conversation. It was during these discussions that I found out about the political unrest that was brewing. I felt responsible for some of it personally. It seems like it was the same day I went to the fertility clinic for my results, several bombings took place across the country. All the places bombed were chemical companies, and I felt I may have incited the radical elements when I spoke on the heap. That would figure too; it was a full moon, we got busted, my boys did not swim, and chemical plants were blowing up…the trifecta. I did not mention it as we talked. The owner talked openly and at length about the fears of vulnerability of our government and our way of life. He called it the great fracturing. Like the "safety" glass of a windshield, when it shatters, it breaks into a million little pieces. There have been numerous factors gnawing away at people's patience and tolerance. They are being manipulated into being reactive species, unable to plan and execute. Always ready to jump at the command of their phones or a new poll or trend. Extremely dangerous and scary times. We have weakened our foundation. There were beliefs and behaviors that were strong adhesives and kept us united in spite of differences. People could rally around being American, being human, rally around integrity, and doing unto others… As patience and virtue disappear, scared individuals look to find security in groups. The increase in information and stimulation makes it tough for people to make good decisions and to stand by those choices for a lifetime. Loyalty has become a consumer good. It is more prevalent in branding and in lobbying.

He too spoke of being on the eve of war. The reactive people were simply waiting for the next command. It could be a civil war, a revolution, a religious war, or the saber-rattling of corporations wanting loosened environmental regulations for the plundering of the planet. With total disregard for the future and for life, reactants would line up on either side of an imaginary line drawn in the imaginary sands. Christian is ready to kill Christian; just try to wrap your head around that. I could see if it were a Christian ready to sacrifice for a Christian…but come on…ready to kill. Recently, one mega-evangelical promoted killing a world leader (may have had something to do with the economy?). What "holy" man would have any credibility inciting the breaking of the first commandment? Even the recent president loudly publicized the fact he is a thieving bastard, and our children are still looking up to him as a role model. He is the most powerful man in the world, and he will squeeze them for money and votes. It would be wise to take a pause and look overseas to see who would benefit the most from this fracturing. The alarm has been sounding, and all the elements, radical or not, stand by, poised to bathe in their countries blood. Apparently, there is no tolerance for freedom, and no freedom to tolerate.

"I came here and started a good life, escaping all the violence in my hometown. I prayed to God that my family would be safe here; now I just do not know," he said that, shaking his head.

This was one of the most American meals I had ever eaten. I felt scared, brave, and frankly reactive, for I was hurt by his sorrows. The play had been written, but they were still in the process of casting. I was hoping I would miss it when it opened, but I was guessing I would be an extra or have some insignificant part. I told him I spend most of my time cleaning up the Garden of Eden. It is decent work; it is the Lord's work. People may come and go with general disregard for the place they are in, and at the end of the day, they realize that this is the place that is the God-given gift to all the life that it supports. Should we go to war? I will be cleaning up, the best I can. We thanked him for the excellent food and conversation and wished him and his family well.

Newday, and I slept out under the lights that night. We had hoped to get over to Oakland, but time just flew by. Tomorrow we would get down the road. The next morning, we woke up early and went to Marina Green. Years ago, I had been there to fly kites. It was therapeutic and calming, and I wanted to get myself into that headspace before we ventured to Oakland. So, we got kites and flew them along the side of the bay. You could see the billows of smoke still rising to the north and east and the Golden Gate Bridge to the north and west. The onshore breeze kept us staring at the darkened skies above Richmond, and I prayed for the strength needed to go into the lion's den. I was telling Newday about the Wild Man of Borneo and Oofty Goofty when some of the Sisters of Perpetual Indulgence passed by along the bay front, adding color to our visit to San Francisco.

Later that day, we made it over to Oakland. Being somewhat familiar with the city, I had an idea of where we could lay low for a spell. Walking past the tagged windowless warehouses on the paved and leaded landscapes to some open spaces. Butts, syringes, broken bottles, paper cups, plastic lids, plastic bottles, pieces of tire, and discarded articles of clothing met with the industrial waste of rusted iron and broken blocks of cement, continuing clear off the land mass and into the bay with decaying piers and shards of metals. Angry or ignorant, the cars flew by. Tatted zombies defying death pushed back against the day. Horns, sirens, and pounding bass hid the songs of the tweaked shorebirds. In a bield among the wind-blown cypress, we made a camp on the cusp of civilization. Together, we made a burnt offering. Together, we dreamed. The weight of the world seemed insignificant compared to the burden of the universe. We slept comforted in the palm of the Lord.

The morning had brought us back to a day with a full moon, which would be overseen with caution and reserve. We picked up trash after finishing off the granola. Stashing our gear, we headed toward Berkeley. Before we could make it past a convenience store, we were lured in by thirst. Whether it was the toxins or the moon, a bipolar rage was building angst and whittling away at my inhibitors. There was not one item in the inventory that was fit for any biologic organism. Newday and I attenuated Rock Stars and laughed at our growing rage.

"How much for a carton of Camel Filters?" I asked.

"Eighty-four eighty-nine," he responded with a thick foreign accent.

"I will take two and these couple things." Pointing to four more Rock Stars I had placed on the counter.

"That will be one hundred and ninety-one and twenty-seven." After taxing and ringing it up.

Outside the store, away from the view of the proprietor, I started opening the packs and placing the tobacco in a neat pile. I picked up the filters and the wrappers —cellophane, foil, paper, and all —and threw them in the garbage. The pile was so depressingly small, and I poured some energy drink on it. Unsatisfied back into the store, all pumped up, I asked for four more cartons. Growing more agitated, I returned to my pile of plant matter and continued my building. I sent Newday in, and she played "Hey Mister" and came out with a load of rolling tobacco. Bugler, Tops, Export, and the like in pouches, bags, and tins, and it all made the mound more substantial. We had spent over a thousand dollars, and Quixote was but a speck on the horizon. Again, it was doused in Rock Star and Red Bulls, and I went back inside.

"Six more cartons," short of breath and anxious I demanded.

By now, a few people had observed the strange behavior, enjoying watching this crazy idiot throwing his money away. One guy even asked for a smoke, to which I replied, "These aren't for smoking!" The pile was still not that big, but you could now see it from the far side of the parking lot. When we went back in this time, I asked for two cases of cartons. Then back to our domestic and Turkish-blend mound. As I worked on the second case, a cop rolled in and had a problem with the small crowd we were attracting. Absorbed in my mission, back in I went. Several others now were willing and anxious to spend time and money, if only for a fleeting second, purifying paradise.

"This is the plague!" I spoke as I ripped up another pack of cigarettes, dumping the tobacco on the pile.

"Tobaccism is one thing…intentionally poisoning tobacco is nothing short of murder. May the souls of the facilitators be blackened and damned for eternity (and I should talk, as my robe was blackened with the sin of judgment). It was with broad strokes that the populous stained. It was the voters, lawmakers, farmers, farm workers, support industries, tobacco companies, executives, and shareholders, part of the medical community, distributors, store owners, stockers, and clerks, and those company shareholders, insurers, advertisers, and their companies and shareholders, and the consumers, and back again to the bankers, lobbyists, and lawmakers who sold the plague, the contagious infection, back to its trusting constituents. And for every dead or dying comrade, two of his comrades were occupied and engaged in the battle. This from the first world: compassionate, Christian, educated, the very pinnacle of the free world, disconnected from life itself, burying guilt and denying remorse. We have the superior moral compass, and we have the pristine future that our dreams pursue. We must navigate into our collective future, pure in thought, pure in body, and pure in spirit. Honoris ante oeconomica!

The crowd had grown to a substantial number, and a local news team showed up and was broadcasting live. A heavier presence from law enforcement was also visible. One police officer grabbed me by my robe and was dragging me toward his vehicle. I did not know why he seemed so mad, but he was spitting as he was saying, "I am going to have to write you up."

"For what?"

"Littering for one," he barked. "We will see what other charges we can add to that."

"I picked up all the trash…the papers, the filters, wrappers, cellophane, and foil!" I spoke.

"That pile was not there before."

They were having trouble with a few dissidents who continued destroying packs of cigarettes when a female officer rudely suggested violence, telling me I had better get my friends to stop. I told her I do not know one person here other than Newday.

"Go twiddle your dew claws!" I snapped back.

Remaining uncooperative when the now-arresting officer was writing me up. "I switched my long-distance carrier to a bag lady with Tourette's syndrome; she screams explicit details of my love for family and friends. Twenty-four, seven, and I enjoy the benefits of free roaming."

No sooner was I cuffed and in the back of a patrol car.

"Name?"

"The Attenuating Puritan," I said sincerely, but it did not fly. And I was brought down to the police station and thrown in jail.

I thought the charges were weak and when I got before the judge, he agreed, and I was dismissed. We went back to camp and prepared ourselves for the next chapter of our lives. Again, we made offerings to God and commitments to each other. What was a purely physical attraction to the young and beautiful Newday grew into a genuine, unconditional love. She also had fallen in love with me and was not casually seeking to experiment with relationships or sex. She had become a good companion, a good wife, and a faithful follower of the Lord.

Her bright blue eyes always filled with eagerness, and her smile encouraging and enticing. Her wild, long, dirty blond hair unassumingly seductive. Her sensual voice was open and honest. I had come to revere her, and together we celebrated our wholeness. Our next adventure would test our compatibility and our faith in the Lord. There would be no turning back, no escape. There were no playing games with each other or in our mutual love for one another. As God as our witness, we said vows. Disregarding what Paul Reubens had once said, "I am a loner and a rebel," I pledged my allegiance to the scorching girl from Burning Man.

It was about seventy-two hours later that we made it over to Berkeley. My search for a geneticist ended at a lab that Doctor Tim had told me about. Dropping names, I was soon introduced to Doctor Wood. She had a long resume and had been involved in many breakthrough research projects, some remarkably similar to what I had been directed to pursue. My faith assured me there was no failure. Persistence and purpose kept the lights burning late. Doctor Wood initially contested some of the experiments. All her life she had served for the betterment of life on earth, and though there was some conflict in her professional ethics, she was soon persuaded by her own altruistic and humanistic instincts.

The civil unrest was escalating. Religious groups had been arming themselves and building militias. Fighting for religious freedom, freedom of speech, or any other kind of freedom was all merely an afterthought. The church leaders were, like everyone else, primarily concerned with economics. Pushing consumerism as the miracle cure of all the world's woes. Bombings continued, and the pushback against consumerism was gaining strength. The economy was faltering. People lost faith in the government and its ability to maintain cohesiveness. Besides the bombings, even more of a precipitating factor was a string of gruesome deaths that got complete media coverage and ostracized the sympathizers of corporate reforms. Protections under the law had allowed corporations to remain unaccountable for untold deaths and diseases. When cornered, shareholders would agree to pass the fiscal responsibility back to the consumer. Lawyers defending the likes of Monsanto, for instance, or big tobacco like Phillip Morris, or Dow and the Atomic Energy Commission would be engaged in the business of putting dollar amounts on human lives while not bankrupting the business or impeding cash flows. Some of these attorneys got paid huge sums to sit in the crosshairs as they became corporate martyrs. One of these attorneys was skinned alive, and his body was reskinned with salted dollar bills. Another had his pockets filled with nickels and was tied to a pier at low tide. Some were forced to consume the perfectly safe products they advocated for, dissolving, or plasticizing them. Corporate mouthpieces suffering the same fate as Parker and Boyd. The radical elements boiled with rage and competed to find punishments that fit the crimes. Exaggerating justice and indelibly staining those original good intentions. With every tick of the clock, further into darkness.

Doctor Wood, Newday, and I suffered several setbacks as we worked diligently on our project. We were under constant threat. We had no guarantees that the resources we needed would still be available. There were no assurances that any of us would be here tomorrow. I kept my faith and renewed theirs in weakness, saying the Lord told me to do this and he will have it done. It is funny how time can move at different speeds at the same time. Now as every second seemed painfully overextended, the days turned into weeks to months in what seemed to be the blink of an eye. We now had secured the species, isolated cultures, extracted and translated DNA, and found the cornerstones of a new life form. With the help of, all things, a herpes virus, these new tools or gifts were given unto me. Though they did not work at first, we continued splicing genes found with similar operons and promoters. Before long, I was a new man. I thanked the Lord for his guidance and his unconditional love.

Time had been running out. I wanted more than anything to do something normal, like fill up some trash bags. At this point, Marshall Law was declared, and it became increasingly difficult to move around. The military had too weakened substantially and were consumed with not only domestic threats but very real foreign threats. The commanders found few taking orders, and with fickle barrels pointed in all directions, loyalties were tested moment by moment. Business remnants vied for protection. Uncivilized mobs burned and looted, raped, and pillaged from sea to shining sea. Some of the mega corporations became small kingdoms and dumped their fortunes into standing armies. Corporate peasants sold themselves for food and became fodder for the consolation prize, the home game of military industrialists. At this point, ninety percent of manufacturing ceased, …which is no way to go to war or defend yourself. No foreign country would ship supplies or aid and wait like wolves, like vultures to make claim to the waste. There were still a large number of people who did not want war. Some of those still had faith in the old ways and were vulnerable to the corrupt abuses of the politico alphas. Others wanted to believe this too shall pass. Beliefs became hopes and wishes.

Newday and I felt we had made substantial progress and decided to take a couple day break from our hurry up and wait routine. One of Doctor Wood's lab assistants were heading over the bridge, and we thought we would spend a day or two on the ocean. Up from the Marin Headlands there is a place called Pirates Cove, and that is where we made our destination. Uncertainty in the city made this a popular spot, but we were determined to get some rest and relaxation. It was nice to be sporting a trash bag and getting back to my feelings of being useful. The ocean was spectacular, and the vistas were breathtaking step after step. Wind-blown cypress shielded us from the onshore gales as they had sheltered others, as was evident from the debris. Naturally, we could not be at Pirates Cove without encountering some pirates. That first night, as we slept, three marauders entered our camp. They were wearing headlamps, and one wielded a machete. The older, toothless one was obviously in charge and demanded something to eat. I told him we did not have much, but he wanted to see just what we had.

"Where you come from?" he asked.

"We just came over from Berkeley," I said.

"Is it still burning over there?" he asked.

"Yeah, parts of the city are on fire. A lot of military over there. They are stopping everyone asking for identification," I said as I reached into a small fanny pack and pulled out some little pieces of plastic that I put in my mouth and ate. Seeing that, one of the other guys, a short, round guy with red hair who went by Frets, grabbed the fanny pack, and ate a small handful of the little tabs.

"Gimme that," the captain scolded, and he also grabbed a handful and ate them. He was at least courteous enough to offer the third member of the party a small ration. I believed they thought they would be tripping within the hour, and I wanted to use that to my advantage.

"She's yours?" asking about Newday, the captain asked.

"Yes!" I said nervously.

"She is fine. Stand over here. Right here, next to The Captain," he said with his toothless grin.

"We both just got herpes over in Berkeley," I said hoping to dissuade him.

"I have every disease known to man. I ain't scared," he said, laughing.

I admit I was nervous myself; rape in the Bay Area is not safe for him or her, Xem or Zé. Any port in a storm.

"Keel hull him and prepare the wench for a fortnight in the forecastle," he said lustfully and lustily.

He was rubbing the flat of the machete blade on her breasts and running his other hand through her hair. "You have got a lot of work to do, but you are young and pleasing to the eye. I may just keep you all for myself. You would like that, wouldn't you?" he said as one eye appeared to float out on him.

Frets came up from behind her and grabbed her ass and squoze it hard with both hands, and she gave a disgruntled aaaarrrrrrgh, which further excited the pirates.

I was still on the ground, and I yelled, "Keep your hands off of her; leave her alone!" My robe was turning a black I did not know existed. The guy behind me must have heard something about the Puritan as he seemed to back off and want no further part of the heinousness the captain would enjoy. The Lord went from rusty red on a white background to the heavy metal look of rusty red on black. I got on one knee and was ready to stand when Frets tried with all his might to kick me in the head, and at the same time the captain swung the machete with lethal force in my direction and severed the right Achilles tendon of Frets. Frets fell to the ground, screaming and bleeding like the stuck pig he was. Newday stepped back behind me, and in a fearless moment, I secured the machete.

"You're that guy," the quiet one said. "I didn't mean nothing."

I ran the machete over the captain's nose and privates and said, "Don't you have a plank to walk? Better get to it! Better yet, get this guy to a doctor before I am forced to do something none of us would appreciate."

In the night, they disappeared. Frets had no use of his foot and needed to be supported, and you could hear the cursing fade as they made distance. Newday was traumatized, and we prayed and made offerings. I told her we were protected as we were doing the Lord's work, and even though she knew it was true, it was still too close for comfort. Aside from our own safety and well-being, these were a few souls that needed prayers, and one of them was injured severely. As we prayed together, our trauma turned into strengths in our faith and in ourselves. We even had the thought that if the Lord wanted us to be the victim, victim it is…but we knew we could not get his work done that way.

We stayed for another two days and walked along the beach, looking at rocks and studying the ocean waves. The onshore breeze invigorated us, and we grew anxious to get back to the work at hand. We did not need too much time off, just enough to remember who we were and what we were doing. Those two days were quiet, and we knew they may be some of the last of the days we would stand on American soil. We are proud to be Americans even when America falters; our dreams, our fantasies, and our nightmares all draped beneath the flag. The subtle changes in the scent of the trees filled me with a need to defend and protect them. Dendronic pheromones jumped species boundaries and cried to us for help. Though the signals were extra loud and clear, I spoke with them about the urgent mission I was on and that I would be back to help when I could. I also told them I would alert some of my own species to make sure their pleas were heard. It was a sad note to be leaving on, and I wondered how many of the forest trees were screaming, running in place, begging for help. Newday and I made offerings and said prayers. We assured the trees, they too, were in the palm of the Lord's hand.

The trip back to Berkeley was perfect. We had walked back to the Black Sands Beach and managed to catch a ride on a boat across the bay. It added new dimensions to traveling about the bay area, and I wondered why I had not previously taken to the waters in an area called the "bay" area. The views were stunning, and the sense of freedom was so much more than driving the diamond lane with the stereo blasting. You were that speck that divided the skies from the waters, and somewhere in your core, what was attenuated from the sky would meet what was attenuated from the water. With that thought, I kept my hand in the water and absorbed like a duck in an oil spill.

When we hit shore, we were immediately stopped by military personnel. It was a friendly encounter, and we showed identification and told them we had work to do at a genetics lab in Berkeley. We were allowed to "pass," and I wondered how many were not allowed and where they would go when they disappeared.

When it came time to infect Newday, I realized we had created a new Frankenstein monster. Initially, even I had lapses in faith. That night, before I drifted off, I had thoughts that it was not fear of God or military might that created the bottleneck on the Y chromosomes. I thought of how environmentalism is a peacetime dividend and wondered if this direction in my life was worthy. As I slept that night, the Lord appeared in my dreams, comforting me, readdressing the mission, stressing the urgency and the need to expedite the process. And with that, it was done.

I was so proud of Newday. She was truly one of a kind. The most giving, self-sacrificing woman in the world, and I loved her beyond measure. We said our goodbyes to Doctor Wood and the staff. We told Doctor Wood we would let her know the results at the first opportunity. She had tears in her professional eyes as we parted. The coast was but a short distance from where we were. For several months, we had been gathering supplies and stocking up. We had outfitted a small sailing vessel. Though neither of us had much experience in sailing, we were all in on this adventurous mission. We both knew the Lord had our backs. Now, like Noah with a microscope, keeping two of all the cultures alive in petri dishes or test tubes was part of my new assignment. As difficult as it was for me to be the zookeeper, I knew the other passengers had their faith also.

The Pacific was calm and calming. Now invigorated with manifestations of paradise, we hoarded our wealth as we sailed into sunset after spectacular sunset. Such peace I had never known, inner and outer, Divinity surpassing mere satisfaction and gratification.

Newday asked in a moment of weakness if we would survive, and I confidently said we would not only survive but thrive, for my faith was strong. My robe never blinked, and that relieved her doubts. Even if the chances were not good for us, she could see it in my robe that I honestly believed we would thrive. When she asked if our boat would make it, I told her "Sure" then my robe would tell her otherwise, and the blackened pixels told her I did not believe this to be true. Of course, in one form one life or another, we would live on, and in the back of my mind, I was saying, "The minnow would be lost."

Periodically, the waters would be tested, and it delighted me to discover it was filthy enough to maintain the cultures of methylobacteria and rhizobiotes. We entered the gateway to a promised land here on earth. All we had heard about it was true, but even more so. Out in the middle of the endless ocean, hundreds of square miles of trash the vast emptiness was scarred, violated, and made finite in just a few greedy, self-serving decades. In Berkeley, we were gifted genes from bacteria that would produce petase and mhetase and gave us Puritans the ability to digest plastic. This now was home. Miraculously, Newday was with child, and she was to bear him here in the waste. These, our children would digest plastic. For we are your future; purity through us, Amen.

Though my behaviors occasionally reflect the toxins my forefathers have bequeathed…with every breath…attenuating, with each and every thirst that is quenched…attenuating…and with every gift from thy bounty…attenuating, purity through me, Amen.

www.ingramcontent.com/pod-product-compliance
Lightning Source LLC
Chambersburg PA
CBHW050538160726
48003CB00002B/655